PRAISE FOR MARIANO'S CROSSING

David M. Jessup's award-winning first novel
to which this book is third in the series

Winner of the
Rocky Mountain Fiction Writers Contest

Finalist for
Colorado Book Award for Literary Fiction

Finalist in
Pacific Northwest Writers Contest
and the Santa Fe Writers Project

What a vivid piece of writing! The craftsmanship is most impressive. And the multiplicity of perspectives makes the truth tantalizingly elusive. Great stuff!—Louis Bayard, New York Times bestselling author of *Mr. Timothy* and other historical mysteries

Marlano's Crossing *is a beautiful, exciting, wonderful novel... I couldn't put it down.... It does what good historical fiction should do—places me in what John Gardner calls the 'vivid and continuous dream.'*—Laura Pritchett, recipient of the PEN USA Award and the Milkweed National Fiction Prize, author of *Hell's Bottom, Colorado*

Based on real characters and the mysteries connected with historic events, author David Jessup has woven a mesmerizing tale of people struggling to find their places in the rapidly changing landscape of post-gold rush Colorado.—Page Lambert, author of *Shifting Stars*, featured in *Inside/ Outside Southwest Magazine* as one of the most notable women writers of the contemporary American West.

Fine writing throughout, with many dynamite scenes and fascinating characters. The descriptions of landscape and the natural world are marvelous, and there's a lot of great history here, along with a complex psychological dimension and a touching relationship between the characters.—Paulette Alden, Stegner Fellow, author of *The Answer to Your Question*, winner, Kindle's Best Indie Book Award.

Mariano's Crossing *is smoothly paced and taut with drama. The internal conflicts of the characters pull them all forward through the story to its dramatic conclusion. The major characters are well rounded, each with a unique voice, as well as faults and virtues that determine their paths along the way.*—Teresa Lewis, *Flatirons Literary Review*

A great character driven work of historical fiction!— Meg Wessell, *A Bookish Affair* book review.

Reading this novel set in the Old West, I was reminded at times of two other historical novels, Snow Falling on Cedars *and* The Kite Runner. *Neither of those books are westerns, but they deal with similar themes—racial and ethnic bigotry and relationships across class boundaries. In all three, there is also a thread of menace.* —Ron Scheer, *Buddies in the Saddle* book review.

Historical fiction that reads like a true story. Told from multiple points of view, Mariano's Crossing *is a convincing historical treatment. Each character has his own voice and is so believable the reader is convinced each one told his version to Jessup in person.*—Patricia Stolty, *Chiseled In Rock* book review.

For way too many years, the many incredible accomplishments of the Hispanic community have gone untold. Finally, David Jessup illuminates the life of Mariano Medina, a very important Colorado Hispanic pioneer.

I very much enjoyed reading his historical novel, Mariano's Crossing, and I know you will as well.—Cecil Gutierrez, Mayor, City of Loveland, Colorado.

I loved hearing David Jessup tell the fascinating story and details behind his book Mariano's Crossing. *Just like James Michener's* Centennial, *Mr. Jessup weaves the story about individuals with their own unique personalities, including strengths and character flaws. To say that this is "history come alive" is an understatement. I cannot wait to take one of David Jessup's tours of the locations he describes in the book.*—Susan Dominica, member, *The Breakfast Club* book club.

PRAISE FOR MARIANO'S CHOICE

Mariano's Choice *is one of those rare, wonderful books that sticks in the mind and heart long after you've read the last page. The story, masterfully paced and filled with fascinating historic details, offers an intriguing snapshot of the West through the eyes of characters largely ignored by mainstream fiction: fur traders, Indian captives, dislocated Spanish settlers, horse trainers and trail blazers.*

The underlying themes of honor, compassion, revenge, and the power of love and friendship, transcend setting and genre. The book shines brightly because of a vulnerable, wily, complicated Spanish Mountain Man—one of the most interesting protagonists I've encountered in a long time. Highly recommended.—Anne Hillerman, *New York Times* best-selling author of *Spider Woman's Daughter* and *Rock With Wings.*

David M. Jessup adds flesh and blood to the bones of one of the West's legendary mountain men. Mariano Medina has not one choice, but many, as he stands up to violence and prejudice—and to his own cowardice. He must choose between fear and friendship, safety and honor, and loyalty and love in this tightly wound novel of the Old West.
—Sandra Dallas, *New York Times* best-selling author of *Westering Women* and *The Last Midwife*.

Jessup is a master historian and writer—and this gorgeous novel proves it. What mesmerizes most is the depth of understanding and love of the West, which therefore includes the untold stories, the filling-in of an incomplete history.

In Mariano's Choice, *we discover the peoples who are often minimalized by mainstream historical fiction but which are essential to an understanding and love of the real and varied West. In vivid and gorgeous prose, we encounter the world of the late 1800s and the men and women who literally shaped the West. We also find a tale of love and the power of redemption. History, place, love, forgiveness, healing: this book has it all. I loved it.*
—Laura Pritchett, winner of the PEN USA Award for Fiction, author, *Hell's Bottom Colorado*.

Mariano's Choice *isn't your typical Western. And Mariano Medina isn't your typical Western hero. Rather than fearless and invincible, he is timid, often uncertain, and occasionally cowardly. Medina and other historical Westerners serve author David Jessup well as he spins a gritty, sometimes painful tale of an ordinary man facing unwelcome change as the fur trade era gives way to immigrant wagons and the United States seeks increasing influence on the Mexican frontier.*

This book reveals the Old West through the eyes of a regular frontiersman and the result is a richer, more realistic interpretation than the overwrought, myth-driven view we see in so many Western novels.—**Rod Miller**, three-time winner of the Western Writers of America Spur Award.

Mariano's Choice *continues the saga of Mariano Medina, a man both ordinary and extraordinary. Author David Jessup's fluid, compelling prose takes the reader back to another time, to share Medina's adventures and adversities. I hope someone has the sense to produce this as a mini-series. It's too rich and complex to fit into a two-hour movie.* —**Lucia St. Clair Robson**. *New York Times* best selling author of *Ride the Wind*, and winner of the Owen Wister award of the Western Writers of America.

Mariano's Choice *is a bold story about the west as it existed before the Western, a story about a raw land populated by rugged folk, men and women, native and immigrant, living alone and in community. Jessup's cinematic eye for detail and his gift for gut-wrenching, heart-pounding storytelling pulls us seamlessly into a world of danger, beauty, and unbounded possibility—for success and failure, for betrayal and redemption, for love and hate, and for life and death.*— Gary Schanbacher, author of *Crossing Purgatory*, winner of the Langum Award for American Historical Fiction.

What strikes me first about Mariano's Choice *is David Jessup's writing. Elegant isn't a word one would usually associate with a novel of the 1800s, yet that's the word that comes to mind. Next, I'm taken by the pace of the story, and the authenticity of the characters. It moves, and they're so believable. Finally, the plot is riveting. The historical basis just adds to it. If Mariano's Crossing was an award-winning first effort, Mariano's Choice should join it on the judges' stand.*— Denny Dressman, author of eight books and President of the Colorado Authors' League.

MARIANO'S
WOMAN

David M. Jessup

ISBN# 978-1-941052-40-2 Trade Paper
ISBN# 978-1-941052-41-9 eBook
Library of Congress Control Number:
2020939436

Cover Design: Antelope Design
The back cover photo was taken by L. A. Huffman in 1878
at Fort Keogh, Montana, of Pretty Nose, a Cheyenne Woman.
Courtesy of Montana Historical Society Research Center Archives.

This is a work of fiction. Any references to places,
events or people living or dead
are intended to add to a sense of authenticity
and to give life to the story.
Names, characters and incidents
are products of the author's imagination
and their resemblance to any real-life counterparts
is entirely coincidental.

Pronghorn Press
pronghornpress.org

To Gray Wolf,
Cheyenne elder, healer, and friend.

ACKNOWLEDGMENTS

This book couldn't have been written without the insights and wisdom of my Cheyenne friend, Gray Wolf, an extraordinary historian and re-enactor who has generously shared his lodge and pipes with me during the annual "Native American Week" at Sylvan Dale Ranch in Colorado. These days it is daunting for any author to try to walk in the moccasins of an Indian woman who lived a hundred and eighty years ago. For me, the risk of committing "cultural appropriation" was overcome by my desire to connect with people from a different culture, time and place. Any success in making this connection is due mostly to Gray Wolf's encouragement. Any mistakes I have made are my own.

The "Upside-down Face" scene is one I owe to a storyteller named Gray Owl, a visitor to Sylvan Dale from the Lakota people.

I owe much of the love charm scene to a University of Nebraska book edited by Jay Miller entitled "Mourning Dove, A Salishan Autobiography."

For the history of Mariano Medina, Takánsy and their children, I relied heavily on Zethyl Gates book, Mariano Medina, Colorado Mountain Man. For information about the Flathead people I used The Flathead Indians of Montana by Harry Holbert Turney-High, Coeur D'Alene, Flathead and Okanogan Indians, by Franz Boas and James Teit, and Recollections of the Flathead Mission by Father Gregory Mengarini. The Jesuit missions to the Flathead people are described in Come, Blackrobe, by John J. Killoren, and Father Peter John DeSmet, Jesuit in the West, by Robert C. Carriker.

Thanks also to my diligent critique readers, Kim Johnson, Eva Talmadge, Liane Norman, Carol Sether, and my patient wife of fifty-four years, Linda Jessup, herself an author of Parenting with Courage and Uncommon Sense, who read my drafts aloud during our morning coffee time, enabling my ears to hear what my fingers had typed.

The back cover photo was taken by L. A. Huffman in 1878 at Fort Keogh, Montana, of Pretty Nose, a Cheyenne Woman, courtesy of Montana Historical Society Research Center Archives. Although the image is not of a Flathead woman, it evoked in me the spirit of Takánsy as I imagine her.

MARIANO'S
WOMAN

1

The Crossing

My body, she is feeling lighter today. Not floating, but almost. I check my feet. They are where they should be, thrust into my old worn-out moccasins, planted on the floorboards of our house. My eyes see, but my no-feeling feet ask me whether my eyes are seeing true.

A strange haze-pulse flickers at eye-edge. Purple dark, it flares and fades with each heartbeat, then slowly lifts like morning meadow fog. I shake my head to try to clear it. I am still in our house, by the river. My feet are still on the floor.

The sickness, maybe. I am growing weaker in past days, unable to eat much. My breath is coming harder, so I spend more time on the pallet that I use for my bed. My muscles, they are wasting, bones showing under my hide, skin thin and spotted as that old rag draped over the pump handle.

It is past time to cross over into the Great Beyond. But I cannot. Not yet.

I am standing next to the table in the cooking room of our log house. The iron stove hulks against one wall, the china cupboard against another. Its shelves have empty spaces where blue china cups used to be. Medina dashed them against the wall, enraged after I stole our daughter's body.

She was lying here on this table, my beloved Lena, stiff and cold in the burial shroud I made for her. I could not let him bury her in his cemetery. I remember how, in the dark, with the great storm masking my sounds of escape, I dragged her out of this house and carried her body to the red-cliff ridge to the west. Only my horse knows where I hid her. Medina will never find where she rests.

The front door swings open with its rusty hinge sound. Medina walks in, wipes sweat from his forehead, and hangs his hat on its peg. He turns, stares right at me, through me. I stare back. He still has the anger, but the blind bull fury is gone. He pretends not to see me, brushes past and steps into the next room. He leaves the smell of leather and smoke in his wake, odors that once stirred my desire. We speak few words to each other since Lena's death. Small words only, everyday words. "Mariano, where you leave the cast iron pot?" Or, "I will not be here tonight for supper." Or, "Woman, where are the shirts you beaded for the trading post?"

Anger at Medina still hardens my heart. He sent my Lena to the Denver City school. Put her on the danger path. I know he was trying to help her, having for her his big pride. But forgiveness, I cannot give.

Two winters have passed since I found Lena's body in the river, face and throat splotched red, glossy black hair matted against her cold skin, eyes glazed through half-open lids, arms and legs stiffening in the moonlight. I try to banish that mind-picture, but it claws me awake at night, a demon badger digging a hole in my head. I curse it, burn sage, invoke old chants I learned long ago. I even try holding my broken cross to my heart when the memory comes, chanting the rosary as I click the black beads in my pocket. Nothing helps.

What I hunger for is Lena's spirit-being. In dreams I sometimes see her as she was, riding her black mare in the Denver City parade, slender in the white doeskin dress I made for her, smiling her beautiful smile. But I never see her spirit-being. Where is she? That is the question that haunts me.

Is she in the Black-robe heaven, surrounded by saints, with Jésu and God's angels among the clouds? In Purgatory, having died without last rites, awaiting travel to a better place? Or has she gone to the Black-robe land of fire? No, no, that cannot be, must not be! She had only fifteen winters of age, too young for mortal sins that send one to the land of forever punishment. That hell is where I may go, where I deserve to go. But not my Lena.

Maybe she travels in the Great Beyond of my people, galloping over green meadows on a fine horse, singing and dancing with our ancestors, well-fed, well loved, in the Road of Many Stars. I wish I could believe this were true. But in my heart I am afraid. I feel her spirit is still close by, trapped, waiting. Salish people believe the spirit dead need prayer medicine for traveling to the Great Beyond, a ceremony one year after crossover-day. April 10, 1872. That is what is written in the Catholic Church Book of the Dead, where Father Machebeuf put her name with his black ink stick.

I tried to make ceremony for her at her secret resting place on her first-year crossover-day. I wanted to know where she is going, so I can follow. But I fear I did not make a right ceremony. Maybe my fire was too small. I was afraid a large fire might reveal the location of her body on the red-cliff ridge. Maybe I did not chant enough. Not all the old words would come to me. I have forgotten so much. Or maybe my offerings—a bit of pemmican, her favorite red ribbon, strands of hair from her horse colt's tail and mane, a copy of her otter pouch—were not worthy.

I needed help from the spirit of Otter Woman. A gray jay flew over and perched on one of the stone slabs that hides Lena's body. That bird is common along the Bitterroot River, but almost never flies here along the Big Thompson. So I thought that bird might be the old medicine-woman's spirit. I spoke to it—said her name aloud—but no answer came.

When I was twelve winters of age, Otter Woman told me how to know when a spirit journeys from this world to the Great Beyond. A shift shadow, a hazy presence, a tremble of leaves with no breeze to stir them. Before traveling to the next world, spirits sometimes linger, swooping silently through the night on owl wings or appearing in the bodies of animals. Or even humans. I do not know if this is true, but these things I watched

for during the time since Lena's crossover.
Nothing. Lena's sad spirit may still be hovering
near, restless, troubled. Waiting to journey into
Black-robe heaven, or walk the great log over the
gorge that separates this world from the Salish
Great Beyond.

My only wish, my last wish, is to be with
my Lena in her spirit world, wherever it is.
Otter Woman once told me how, with right spells,
you can speak with spirits, if not in words,
in mind-thoughts. I must speak with my daughter,
explain my false-tongue stories about her young
suitor, John Alexander. She must understand it
was for her own good, so she would escape with
me instead of marrying him. I must try once
more to reach her on the red-cliff ridge so she can
finish her journey to the next world. So I can follow.

I leave the house and walk over the toll
bridge that made my husband wealthy. Mariano's
Crossing, he proudly calls it. The air is warm.
Despite sun-above, the water shimmers dark, clear
but not clear. Strange purple haze wisps around
cottonwood leaves. The river sings its gurgle song,
breathes its mossy odor, familiar sounds and
smells. I walk upstream along the river trail to a
place where a lichen-covered boulder rests beside
the riverbank. I pull away the smaller stones piled
at its base, stones that seem natural to other eyes
but mine. Underneath is the obsidian blade I hid
there after Lena's death. I pick it up by the thick
edge, feel its heft in my palm. It glows, pulsing in
time with the purple haze that throbs at the edges
of my vision. I run my thumb across the thin edge.
Sharper than any knife.

I touch the scars made by the stone on my upper right arm, just below the shoulder. The lowest scar is newest, left there when I pressed the blade into my flesh after Lena's death. The next is for Martin, my youngest boy, barely six winters old when he returned to us dead, tied to the saddle of the horse he was riding to prove his manhood. The third is for my little Rosita, not even a winter old when dying of the weakness sickness.

The last scar I touch is hardened into a rough, aging welt near the top of my shoulder. Punishment for the loss of my first love, long ago, caused by my own willful actions. A story I have never told anyone except Jésu. A story I must tell Lena so she will understand. Heat creeps up my neck even now at the shame of it. I did not want Lena to make the same mistake I did.

The black stone's spirit calls me to press the blade into my throat instead of my arm. I heft the obsidian toward my neck. How easy to push it into the artery, let the blood pulse out in great arcs, let my mind forget all. But first I must make one last try to connect with my daughter's spirit.

I return the obsidian to its hiding place and cover it with stones.

Farther upstream I leave the river to climb the red-cliff ridge. There is no trail here, so I push my way through bushes that leave scratches on my arms. Sweat drips down my face and sides. I feel so weak I wonder if I will be able to reach the top. By the time I arrive at Lena's secret resting place, my legs are shaking, and my breath comes in short gasps. I pull the stopper from my water skin and take a long swallow.

Lena's bones lie under a pile of rocks between two sandstone slabs that lean against each other like lazy sentries. The opening between them, I have covered with a thin piece of sandstone. It takes the rest of my strength to push it aside. The rocks behind it—her rocks—are undisturbed. Good. No bear or wolf or coyote has found this place. Neither has Medina, or the John Alexander boy who was hoping to marry her, or curious settlers.

It is here I made the crossover ceremony twelve moons ago. Here I come every moon to try talking with Lena's spirit. Will this last visit be different? I hope so. My time is short.

I squat in front of the opening, pull a sage bundle from my belt pouch and light it with one of Medina's phosphoros. With a hawk wing I wave smoke in the four directions. I chant Lena's crossover song. I call her name, which you are not supposed to do if you want a spirit to cross over. I don't want that. Not yet.

Sun travels across the sky from sun-above halfway to sun-asleep. I try praying to Jésu. I make the Catholic touching sign. I feel the broken rosary in my pocket. No response. Not a surprise, since I cursed the name of Jésu after finding Lena's body. But I am willing to try anything for a chance to find her spirit-being.

I rise, defeated. I take in the vast sky, the shining white peaks toward sun-asleep, the river far below snaking from canyon mouth through sandstone ridges that flank the great mountains. Purple haze still flutters at eye-edge, but dimmer now. Pine scent rides the air I breathe, the squawk of a black-headed blue jay and the trill of a meadowlark reach my ears. The buzz of bees. These are things of this world I will miss. Along with my children.

I turn slowly in a complete circle. No sign of Lena's spirit-being. I sigh, replace the sandstone that hides her resting place, and turn to leave.

I step lightly downslope, watching for prickly pear and rattlesnakes. Below, the river winds toward the Crossing, cloaked in green cottonwoods.

Sudden silence. At the far side of eye-edge, I see something move. A chill comes over me. A figure appears from behind a juniper tree. I stare. My breath catches. My heart races. A cry rises in my throat.

It is her.

Her hair is glossy black, the shine back in it. Color is in her cheeks. She is wearing the white doeskin dress I spent a full summer beading for her, the dress she wore while riding Shy Bird in the Denver City parade. She is as beautiful as I remember her.

She turns away to face the western mountains and raises her arms toward the sun. White leather fringes spill against her tawny arms. My beautiful daughter. Her spirit-being, found at last!

I am afraid to breathe, but must, or faint. I take in a small breath, let it out slowly, slowly. Dare I call to her? I fox-step in her direction, balancing on a flat rock. Then another. A breeze touches my face. A scent of freshly turned earth. Her scent? I am downwind of her. If she were a deer she would not catch my scent. But she is not a deer.

Another step. The rock tips, clicks against another. Lena lowers her arms, slowly turns toward me.

No! Her eyes are vacant gray orbs, staring at nothing. Unseeing ghost eyes.

A cry escapes my throat. I fall to my hands and knees and scrabble backwards, stop, look up. Her dead eyes rove over me, no-see eyes. Not her real eyes, which were dark brown, lovely. They are like my own gray eyes, my ghost eyes that stare back at me when I look at a mirror. Then she turns away, steps—or floats—behind the juniper tree and fades from view.

"Lena!" I push myself off the ground and rush forward. "Lena, do not leave me!" I shove the juniper branches aside, scramble around, searching, calling out. She is gone. So close. Was it a vision? An awake-dream brought on by lack of food, sickness? Is my mind failing?

I return to the tree. A scrap of red ribbon lies on the ground where she stood. I pick it up, feel its weave, pinch it, marvel at its unfaded redness. It is real.

I sit down, clutching the ribbon. Maybe she will return. I wait, head turning this way and that at every mouse rustle in the grass, every bird flitting through bushes, every breeze moaning through sandstone rimrock.

As I wait, my heart sinks. Is Lena warning me away? Telling me not to follow her? Does she blame me for what happened? That must be it. Giving me a sign that we will travel separate roads to the Great Beyond.

I clutch the ribbon. "Lena, my child. Come back." I cringe at the sound of my voice, the desperate wail of it. I clamp my hand over my mouth. I breathe, trying to rein in my galloping heart. To reason with myself. Maybe she is still around. Maybe she can hear my thoughts even if I cannot see her. I will sit here, tell my story. Maybe if she understands why I did what I did, our spirits can join.

2

STAYS WITH HORSES GIRL

Lena, my daughter, hear me. You know me as a quiet one, a mother with heart for you and your brothers, working long days for making beadwork on *camisas* for your father to sell at trading post. Making beautiful dresses for you, for when you made peoples' eyes go round seeing your spirit power with horses. You know me as one who loves horses but never rides them. You have asked me for why, and I always turned you away with short answers about my vow to Jésu.

Now I tell you the "for why" of my vow.

The way you knew me was not always my way. Your mouth will fall open to hear that as young girl, I loved racing horses and hated beadwork. Among my people, the Bitterroot Salish, this made me strange. Every other young girl learned the woman's-way: skinning hides, chewing leather to make soft, sewing pants and *camisas* and dresses, weaving baskets, preparing food, moving and setting up lodges. Beadwork was big, and women were trying to get *eee's* and *aaah's* for best designs, best patterns, best tightness of bead rows.

Most of this woman's-way you never had to learn. At Mariano's Crossing we get goods for money trade. But among my people, we had to make almost all things for living. Doing these things did not fill my heart. When working on them my mind would wander off to the horse meadow. I made mistakes, dropped beads, spilled things, pricked myself with needles, not the metal kind you know but needles of bone.

My older sister, So-chee, was the best among girls learning beadwork. She was pretty, not tall and thin like me. When she walked past boys, tight braids swinging side to side in time with her hips under too-tight dresses, young men's eyes popped out of their heads. Her eyes would crinkle-laugh, so pleased with herself.

Aunt was pleased with her, too. Aunt was the one who taught us the beading. With So-chee she had a quick learner. With me she had a slow one. Once I heard them talking about me after I left the beading lesson and stepped outside the lodge. Aunt said no boy will want me if I cannot make good *camisas* and leggings and moccasins. So-Chee laughed, and said hurt-words I cannot forget: "No boy will want her because she is so skinny. And they are afraid of her eyes!"

I remember that laugh and how it made my face burn. I could get more plump by eating more, but my eyes could not be changed. Their pale gray reflection in water's still surface reminded me: I am not like other children.

"She will fatten up one day," Aunt said, ignoring the eye comment. "Now she is too busy with horses to eat."

So-chee laughed. "The last moccasins she made—one is too small for her foot, and the beads! Eeee! They droop down on one side like a child put them there. She is ten winters old already."

Aunt wanted my sister to help me learn, but So-chee refused. In a cold voice, she told Aunt that other girls laughed at me behind their hands. "They call her 'Stays-with-Horses,'" she said. "It bothers me, their laughing, so I laugh with them."

Her words gave me heart-fall. Three winters older, So-chee had thoughts only on boys, her *amigas*, her place in our band. Mine were on horses. I made my heart hard against her and her friends. Made myself glad for her cruelty because it allowed me more time with horses.

Most people in our band thought me strange. I agreed with them, which is why I went to the horses at sun-awake and sun-asleep, when most people were eating and not noticing me out in the horse meadows beside the river.

Lena, how I wished for you to see our Salish people's horses! That is one reason for why I pushed you to run away from your father, to leave our home at the Crossing and go with me to the land of my childhood. I wanted you to see the Bitterroot meadows. Green waves of grass belly-high during summer moons. Walking through those meadows as a girl always made my heart sing. Smelling fresh morning dew and damp earth. Watching meadow gnats dancing above the grass, tiny sparks lit by sun. Hearing chickadees and tanagers and finches welcoming me.

Your heart would swell at seeing our horses! Sorrels, blacks, grays, paints, a roan and an appaloosa, each picketed on its own tether. I remember their horse smells, their steaming piles of fresh droppings, their satisfied snorts as they tore off clumps of grass to chew. I gave each horse a name. Eats-a-lot for a fat sorrel mare who gobbled grass as if starving, guarding her patch of pasture with bared teeth and laid-back ears. Such a glutton! She was boss of herd, *la Jéfe*.

And there was Shy Bird, the same name as the horse you rode so beautifully when you had only twelve winters. My Shy Bird was black, a mare, like yours, with two white socks. Riding her was having a thunder cloud between my legs. Wind in face, hair blowing, wild freedom.

You know that feeling. That is for why I taught you the horse-riding way, to watch you smile, for you to feel the power of a horse, your control of thunder. How I loved teaching you, so proud I was of your horse-spirit path. How you opened the eyes of the Lightskins who watched you in the Denver City parade!

That is why I worried about your love for the John Alexander boy. I was afraid you would throw away your horse-spirit path and walk the mating-road. Make the same mistake I made. The best for you was what I wanted.

3

IRONHAND

Lena, my flower, if you are hearing me, listen well. To know me you must learn about my father, your *abuelo*.

My Father was fierce, with eagle eyes that pinned me like arrows into crouching silence. The most horses, the finest horses, were his. More than anyone in our band, even our chief.

At council meetings and dance ceremonies, people sang about Father's bravery. Told stories about his one-man attack on three mounted Blackfeet warriors, the mighty swing of his war club that brought them down, his turning back the enemy and saving the people from defeat. This great coup-counting gained him his name. Ironhand. But it left his leg muscles so torn by an enemy spear that he limped for his rest of life.

My girl eyes saw him with pride, as a great man. I always wanted him to see me with proud eyes, too.

Father had four wives, same as chief Big Face, the *jéfe* of our band. Lena, you would be surprised by this because it is not our way at the Crossing. But in the long ago, having more than one wife showed a man had big medicine to be rich, like having many horses. The Catholic Black-robes tried to stop people from taking many wives. A sin, they said. But the Black-robes did not understand that when warriors were lost in battle, leaving more women than men, widows needed help to feed themselves and their children, and good men took them as wives for protection.

Lena, you have only one mother. I had two. My real mother passed into the Great Beyond when she was in the birthing lodge. My own birth caused it. I was too large, my father said. He spoke true. Seeing myself in water reflection always told me of Father's words. My head stuck up taller than others my age.

I still feel the sadness about my mother. There is a dream I had as a girl, over and over. It is dark. I am clinging to my mother's breast, she holding me. Suddenly there is screaming, and I am on the ground. A woman is lying next to me, crying out, reaching for me. A cut in her head bleeds, an unstoppable red flow running down her face, pooling under her eyes. I am desperate to go to her, but I cannot move. My arms and legs are bound. It is useless to struggle. A shadow passes over us as life drains from the woman's eyes and her cries are no more. I am left with her sightless stare, her open, still mouth, and her blood-dripping face. I am growing larger, becoming a huge child. Her death is my fault. I wake up, shaking, afraid, knowing I have failed her.

Father left me to Aunt to raise. Aunt's first husband was killed in a Blackfeet raid before I came into this world. In the custom of our people, my father took Mother's sister as wife. Three other wives ran lodges for him, all with their children. All with higher standing than Aunt.

Aunt had the manner of a cringing puppy. Her hands would flutter like wounded birds, moving from knees to mouth to graying braids. Her eyes looked only at ground. No medicine-power in her. No *sumesh*, as the Salish would say.

Aunt always backed away whenever Father was angry. She watched him like rabbit watches wolf, ready to jump this way or that at his arrow-eye look. Most women ruled their lodges like she-bears in cubbing season. Not Aunt. When Father did not like his food, he yelled and threw it at her. Once he threw boiling stew. Her neck was scarred from that hot stew.

That is another reason for why I avoided Aunt's teaching me the women's-way and refused to obey her. For her, I had no respect, only shame. I did not want to be like her. In mind-thought I saw my dead mother as tall and beautiful, as strong within her lodge as Father was among the warriors. Worthy of his respect, as I wanted to be.

Another surprise for you, my Lena, is telling you how my father beat his wives. My husband, Medina, never beat me, except after your crossover when I stole your body away for burial, so you do not know this kind of father. Among Salish men of the Bitterroot, not all beat their wives, but those who did were not thought wrong.

Once Father hit Aunt so hard she fell to lodge floor like a head-shot deer. I was squatting quietly in back of lodge, seeing her crumpled body, blood dripping from her nose, moccasin dangerously close to center cook fire. Father wiped his knuckles, stormed around shouting curses, kicked her leg and finally left her lodge. My heart should have felt heavy for Aunt, but my girl-self blamed her, thinking Father was right for hitting her. I thought she was like the weak pup in a litter, somehow deserving this. I wanted my father to give me the respect, so he would not beat me too.

The problem was I saw no way to gain his respect in the way girls were expected to.

To Father, we daughters were supposed to be good in the women's-way, to find husbands from good families. He wanted his daughters to be pretty, like So-chee, to make young men eager to want us as brides. To make better bride gifts. Bride gifts were usually horses, but scarce black powder weapons would be even better. Father's brief glances at me, eyes quickly sliding away, told me of my low bride-gift value.

Still, during my year of ten winters, I decided to try. I forced myself to sit inside Aunt's lodge with the black hand painted on the side, fingers pointing up, the sign of Ironhand, and did my best to learn Aunt's teaching the women's-way. Stitching, tanning, weaving and beading while Aunt fluttered and fussed. So-chee worked faster and better. Her friends *eeeeh'd* and *aaaah'd* when they saw her beadwork; laughed behind their hands when they saw mine. So I knew there was no way for me to please Father in the same way as So-chee.

During this time my mind would wander

back to the horses, like a puppy who cannot resist stealing fresh meat. The horse-spirit path was strong in my bones, like you, Lena. While sewing on a bead, I would wonder if a sick horse was healing, if willow leaves were a good remedy for horse colic, if Shy Bird was faster in the racing than other horses. I was feasting on thoughts about learning to race, about riding my horse better than others, about crossing the finish line first.

Stop thinking about these questions, I told myself. But the thoughts would not leave me. I was mind-dreaming of Father's seeing me with proud eyes.

4

THE CLIFF

Telling Lena about Father jolts me out of my story. I am still sitting on the red sandstone ridge next to where I saw Lena's spirit-being. I glance around, hoping she has heard me. Hoping she will return.

I recall telling Lena why she should leave Mariano's Crossing, why she should forget her rag-clothed young suitor, John Alexander, and come with me to the Bitterroot instead, for her own good. Why she must continue her horse-spirit path, seek honor and fame as a horse woman rather than throwing it all away on too-early mating. Why she must escape the Denver City school that Medina forced on her.

She died an innocent. I will die a sinner. For many years I believed in forgiveness. Now I think there will be no forgiveness for me. That I will go to a different afterworld than she.

I lean back against a flat stone and close my eyes. Talking to Lena has drained my energy. Cloud shadows drift across my lids as overhead juniper branches wave in the breeze. Sleep beckons.

A dark shadow falls across my face. A sudden coldness surrounds me. I try to keep breathing, slow, steady. Keep my heart from racing. Pretend to sleep. Slowly I open my eyelids a tiny slit. Through my lashes I see two eyes peering at me. Dark centers rimmed in yellow. A figure is leaning over me. I can no longer pretend sleep.

"Hello daughter," it says in a low, throaty rasp.

A scream escapes my throat as I roll to the side and scramble up on my hands and knees.

His lips curl back into a familiar, yellow-tooth smile with one missing long-tooth. Three eagle coup-feathers point skyward from his head. A black blanket shrouds what I remember are powerful shoulders. Long nose, sloping forehead, wolfish face. And the eyes! The same arrow eyes that shot into me as a young girl.

"Father?"

The smile widens, inviting. The eyes grow friendly. "Yes. You know me. It is good."

Part of me is happy. My father—his spirit-being—has sought me out. The same hunger for his attention that burned in me as a young girl floods into me. But I wonder, what does he want?

As if reading my mind, he says, "I can take you to her."

I rise to my feet, heart pounding.

He backs away, motioning me to follow. Step by step he moves upslope. I move with him, as if pulled by invisible sinew, over flat sandstone rocks fringed with bunch grass and scattered mountain mahogany bushes toward the rimrock cliff that overlooks the river valley far below. My heart swells with new hope. Lena! He will take me to her. He knows where her spirit lives.

"Where? How long will it take?"

"Not far. She is waiting for you."

His limp is gone. He is young again, from a time before I was born. His motions are fluid, wolf-like. Swinging at his side is the great war club that gave him his name: Ironhand.

Still backing up, he arrives at the cliff edge. Without a pause he steps off.

"Father, no!" I reach for him.

But instead of falling to the rocks below, he hangs suspended, walking on air.

I stop, astonished.

"Come, my daughter. Do not be afraid. We are at the doorway. Your beloved Lena awaits."

His voice sounds sincere, hinting of father-love I always hoped for as a child. He beckons with his hands, urging me forward.

I walk to him, drawn toward the cliff edge. One step, two steps and I am there. My foot accidentally dislodges a small stone which falls over the edge. It does not float. The sound of its clatter on the rocks below sends a warning. I pause, one foot suspended over the abyss. The hairs on my neck rise.

"You are almost there. Come." Father reaches out to take my hand with his hand. The skin on his arm and hand is now almost transparent. Through it I see a yellow claw. Shocked, I draw my hand away.

"Give me your hand!" His voice is suddenly harsh, demanding. "Step forward or you will never see her again." Gone are the kind eyes and beguiling smile. Rimmed again with glowing yellow, his pupils become slits. His nose morphs into a dark beak. The black blanket becomes two wings as it slips away from his head revealing a blood-red bald skull with no ears. The creature wheels away on an updraft, turns in a great circle and sweeps toward me, claws outstretched, its rasping cry no longer human.

I fall back, scrabbling away from the cliff edge, my own screams mingling with the screech of the huge vulture creature that wheels away into the sky, spirals up in preparation for another dive. I spring to my feet, ignoring the pain in my knees, and stagger downslope toward Lena's leaving place. I trip, crash to the ground. A sudden pain in my head, and everything goes black.

5

THE CHASM

Ironhand curses his bad luck. Almost I had her, he thinks, glancing at his talon, useless against the living. One more step, a death plunge, a crossover. Defeated, he wheels away on black wings toward the in-between world. With no trees to perch on, he flutter-falls to the sandy ground, careful to avoid the cholla cactus sentinels reaching for him with their detachable spiny fingers.

He peers across the chasm that separates him from the Great Beyond, that far-side place of lush grass, plentiful game, forever spring, magnificent race horses. The place where his ancestors live, his band of the dead. He imagines being there, basking in the admiration of the people, brandishing his mighty war club, feasting on fat buffalo hump, fucking his wives, singing his battle victories, humiliating any who challenge him. Winning horse-racing bets. His mind aches, wishing for it.

On the other side of the chasm, crouching by the end of the cross-over log, Guardian Wolf stares back at him, great yellow eyes glowing, saliva dripping from its huge jaws, tongue lolling like a monstrous pink slug between pointed fangs. The god-cursed beast never sleeps. Ironhand has tried every way to get past him. Bribery, flattery, threats. Shape-shifting into a vulture to fly over the chasm, only to smack into an invisible wall that sends him plummeting back to the dry desert floor.

"Let me pass!" he roars, shaking the war club they buried with him. The beast smiles its god-be-damned smile and repeats its god-be-damned reply: "Pass the pipe."

Pass the pipe? Ironhand is sick of hearing this. What the fuck-dog does it mean? Back in the long-ago when he was still in the land of living, a pipe would be passed at council meetings, marriage gift exchanges, peace talks. At betting circles before a horse race. It was supposed to create peace-promise, a pledge of no attacks, a no-lie bargain. A trust-bond.

Not that he would always use it that way. In his hands, the pipe passing helped him fool unsuspecting opponents, trick Lightskin traders into bad bargains, lull unwary horse owners into placing bad bets. No woman-soft pipe-passing for him.

A mind-flash comes to him. A memory of his young ten-winter self. He is cradling a yellow-haired she-pup in his arms, smiling at her whimpering tongue-licks, her eager face, her trusting eyes. A looming father shadow, a bone handle of an obsidian blade thrust toward him, a hard command: "Kill it." A horrified panic, forbidden revulsion, white flash of dread. And finally, after a too-long pause, a knife thrust into an unsuspecting throat, a gush of blood, a stain spreading on his leggings like an unstoppable spring flood. Worst of all, tears. Despite desperate eye squeezing, they leak out anyway, undeniable evidence of his weakness, laid bare for his brothers to witness, his father to see. He cringes before the expected beating, but what comes is worse. The low taunt of his Father's voice: "Go help the women pick berries. You will never walk the warrior path."

He shakes away the memory.

The beast's demand to pass the pipe makes no sense here in this forsaken desert. *No one is here to pass the pipe with me! Doesn't the stupid beast understand this? The other people-dead are in the Great Beyond. How can I pass the pipe if I cannot cross over to them?*

Even if he could, his mind rebels at the idea of pipe-passing with such people. Is he supposed to make peace with the enemies he has killed? The fools he has bested in horseracing? The wives he has justly punished for their stupid blunders, like Takánsy's mother? The moccasin lickers who tried to win his favor? The thought turns his stomach.

What about the living? They can be watched but not touched, he has learned. They do not see or hear the dead, at least not him. They ignore his shouts, threats, smiles, friend offers, his futile efforts to thrust a makeshift pipe into their hands.

He knows he cannot return to the land of the living. He has tried. How many times has he spread his black wings to cruise the shadowy edges of in-between-world where people sometimes wander when they are about to die? Once he spotted Snow-Cave Man there, the too-good Black-robe follower who had poisoned his daughter's mind. They could have passed the pipe if Snow-Cave Man were brought over. But that old cripple would not be lured into a cross-over even when he, Ironhand, offered to adopt the Black-robe religion. *Hai! That would have been a joke!* But Snow-Cave Man shrunk away as if Ironhand had the red-spot disease! Disappeared in a fog-haze!

He shape-shifts from vulture back to human form and paces between the lurking chollas. In this wasteland his body reverts to old-man form. His stick-thin arms swing at his sides, shadows of their former warrior-strong shape. His man-parts ooze pus sickness. His crippled leg drags in the sand. His insides ache from too much Lightskin firewater, the big medicine he love-hates for weakening him unto death. In the Great Beyond his body will regain warrior strength. He must find a way to get there.

His thoughts return to his near-miss with Takánsy, his worthless strange-eyed daughter, on her wobble legs. *So close!* He almost had her with his offer to lead her to her own daughter, his granddaughter. Lena, she has named her. Her neediness to find Lena is a good hook for a hungry fish. Something to lure her over the edge, even though he has no idea of where her Lena is. If he could talk her over they could pass the pipe. Then maybe that gods-be-damned wolf-beast would let him cross.

He tries to imagine passing the pipe with

Takánsy. She had ruined his biggest horse bet, brought disgrace to him in the eyes of the people. He had beat her, shamed her, driven her out of their village on the Bitterroot. How can he pass the pipe with her? Then, he thinks, she can apologize. *Thank me for not cutting off her nose. That would be a good pipe-passing.*

He drags himself into the partial shade of a withered mesquite and begins to plot his next attempt to lure Takánsy to the other side.

6

NIGHT-RIDER

I jolt awake. I am lying on the hard sand and flat stones of the red-cliff ridge where I fell while running from Father's spirit-being. I shake myself, sit up and cast about for the black-winged creature. The sky is empty. Two sparrows flit through the bush beside me. A lizard blinks at me from its rock perch. A bee bumbles on the petals of a yellow flower. All is as it was.

Was the vulture-father another dream? I tell myself it was. But as I run my fingers through my hair I discover a lump that was not there before.

My fall was real at least. A shudder ripples through my shoulders.

I struggle to my feet. Best to leave this place of spirits. But my Lena, she is near. I still feel her presence. I move further downslope, away from the cliff edge and find another tree to lean against. My story, I must finish.

My throat is dry, sore from aloud-speak. Tree bark digs into my back, and stone presses against the bones in my hip, no longer protected by rump flesh. I shift position, drink from my water skin. I wonder if my words have been heard by Lena's spirit-being. I am weary of trying to reach her with my voice. I sound like raspy hinge. Speaking aloud weakens me. I wonder, do spirit-beings need aloud-speak? Maybe they can hear mind-thought just as well.

My mind recoils at the thought of telling Lena more about my father. Instead I decide to tell her about one who understood my hunger for horses, the old man who stood guard while I practiced the horseracing-way. The one who taught me about Jésu and the Black-robe religion.

Snow-Cave Man.

My heart lifts even now when I think of him. His face was crossed with many age lines, as if each of his fifty winters left its mark. When he smiled, one corner of his mouth rose higher than the other, showing only half his teeth. Some found this strange, but for me, his smile was like warm sun. A welcome face, who listened with full attention, as if my words were worth the hearing.

His walking-way was off-balance, because of his toes. Frostbite took them during his spirit-partner quest when he was young and I not yet born. He was high on Shining Mountain when a sudden snowstorm caught him, wind freezing and howling. His hollowed-out shelter in the snow saved life, but not toes.

Like me, Snow-Cave Man was different. Maybe that is for why I felt close to him. In his case, he walked the road of the Catholic Black-robe religion, even before the Black-robes came to our village. This he learned from Iroquois people while on a journey toward sun-awake after his spirit-partner quest, when he was a youth of eighteen winters. On his return, he carried a small wooden cross and made the Catholic touching sign. He spent much time alone, bowing to the cross and droning prayers. When an Iroquois man named Old Ignácio came to live with our Bitterroot Salish band for several winters, Snow-Cave Man and a handful of others would gather around his lodge to learn the Jésu-way, singing hymn songs and praying together. Later, almost all our people decided to walk the Jésu road. But when I was young, there were few.

Snow-Cave Man did not have wives or children. Because of his bad feet he could not walk the warrior road. Hunting was hard for him. These things, plus his Jésu-way, kept him apart. He often drew curious glances and behind-the-hands talk.

His useful place, his helping-way, was guarding horses. His own herd was small, four or five, but he also helped guard Father's herd of fifty-sixty, often in same meadow. Father trusted him, and Snow-Cave Man did not ask payment for his help. His lodge, a small hide-covered lean-to, was usually set up next to horse meadows as we changed camps along the Bitterroot.

His time as horse-watcher was usually at night, when most men and boys were sleeping. The men kept their best horses, the buffalo runners, war horses and racers, inside the circle of lodges at night, picketed or hobbled next to their owners' lodges. Some warriors stretched a rope from the horse to a dangling rattle-alarm that would awaken the sleeper inside if anyone tried to lead the horse away. The not-so-valuable horses would be pastured in a riverside meadow at night. These were the ones guarded by Snow-Cave Man.

During Berry-picking Moon, when some warriors traveled over the mountains toward sun-awake for the late summer buffalo hunt and our village was less protected against Blackfeet raids, young men would help Snow-Cave Man in the horse-watching. But during late snow and greening moons, when horse stealing was less likely, Snow-Cave Man would circle the pasture by himself, warming his hands on a small fire, guarding against lions and wolves, healing sick or injured horses, and catching any loose horse that pulled its picket and wandered away.

Those are the times I would visit the horse meadows.

I lean back, close my eyes, and time-journey back to the time of my first heart-talk with Snow-Cave Man.

It is early spring of the Greening Moon. I have ten winters of age. The sun is barely starting its sky journey. I am standing beside a palomino I named "Buttercup." Something in the horse's stance—a tenderness, or weakness—draws my attention. I walk over and begin stroking the horse's side and chest, my fingers working their way down toward a golden foreleg.

As I lean down lower, there comes a voice behind me.

"What does Ironhand's daughter think about that horse?"

I jump and turn. Snow-Cave Man stands about five paces away. He favors one leg, hips slanting to one side. One hand holds a tether rope, the other a walking stick. He must have come from the trees on the far side of the meadow. I bow to hide the heat flush on my face and stammer out a Salish greeting: "May the Spirits walk with you."

He answers with a Black-robe greeting. "Jésu be with Thee." Such words are not new to me. Our paths have crossed during other horse visits, and like others of our band, I know about some of his ways from what people say about him.

I look back at the palomino. "Ridden too long, I think...it may be the shin soreness."

He walks around to the other side of the horse, his hand trailing across its golden rump. "How do you know this?" he asks, gazing back at me over the top of the horse's back.

His eyes hold mine in a way that loosens my tongue. "Just a feeling, I guess...I have not yet finished feeling." I reach over to feel the horse's foreleg. Buttercup steps back in pain. "Yes." I say.

"You should find out more about that feeling you get," he says. "You may have a bond with the horse-spirit."

My heart quickens as I look up into his warm eyes. "Do you really think so?"

"You may be able to become a horse healer. When you go on your spirit-partner quest you should see if the horse-spirit comes to you."

His words lift my heart. Only last week I braved Father's glare to tell him that one of his paint mares was coming down with colic. Father, head lost in a stick-gambling game, waved me away. He did not bother to check, and by morning the mare died, thrashing on its back in terrible pain.

I think, if I become a horse healer, Father will hear my words. He will seek my horse wisdom. My mind blooms at the thought. Can horse medicine be mine? Then I remember my woman-way duties, and the smile inside me fades.

Snow-Cave Man, somehow knowing my mind-thoughts, asks, "What troubles you?"

His manner frees my tongue. "Do you think me...am I, well...odd? You know, too...too attached to horses? My Father expects me to follow the woman's-way."

He places his hand on Buttercup's rump and circles back around to face me. "Who are we to deny our Spirit's call? Yours is no different from anyone else's...just stronger."

Without thinking, I grab his hand and pull him toward Shy Bird, who is grazing on the shady side of the meadow.

"Careful." He laughs, stumbling slightly to regain his balance.

Embarrassed, I let go of his hand and skip ahead to Shy Bird's side. She greets me with a soft-nosed nuzzle. I feel like flinging my arms around her neck, but stop myself, remembering to ask her permission first. The sleek black hair on Shy Bird's chest is tufted with a few remaining long hairs, stragglers from the winter past.

"You will soon be shiny all over," I say.

"She runs like the wind." Snow-Cave Man limps up beside me. "The racing spirit is strong in her."

I surprise myself by asking, "Do you have a spirit-partner?" It is a bold question. Not something a girl of ten winters asks a grown man. I watch his face for any sign of annoyance.

He smiles. "Yes, I have a spirit-partner...but it is not an animal spirit."

I hesitate, then ask what it is.

"Jésu."

"The baby they talk about? The Black-robes?" I had heard Father talk about Snow-Cave-man's Black-robe belief in this god baby, but he and most of the other men laugh at the idea.

"Yes. But the baby grew up and died long ago and now his spirit is there for everyone."

"Did you see that baby on your spirit-partner quest?"

"No. That was before I learned about Jésu. But I believe it was He who saved my life...from that." He points up toward the round, snow-capped summit that rises over this part of the valley. "The ice of Shining Mountain."

I plunge ahead, reckless with curiosity. "If you died up there, what would...where would your spirit go?"

He gives me a long look, as if to size up my ten-winter-old ability to understand. "If you believe in Jésu, you do not die. Your spirit lives forever in a place called Heaven. Not a place, really. Not like an encampment on a river or a valley in the mountains. More like a beautiful space full of light where peace and happiness surround you."

"Are horses there? Like the Great Beyond in the Road of Many Stars? Where there is plenty of game, plenty of grass, no hunger, no sickness?"

"Better than that," he says. "Love and happiness beyond what we can imagine."

I wonder about this for a moment. Better than horses?

"What happens if you do not believe in Jésu?"

His face darkens. "The Black-robes say there is another place of burning flames where those who deny Jésu's teachings must suffer after they die."

I must look worried, because he quickly adds, "People who are good and kind do not go there. Their spirits linger in a third space where they have a chance to learn the Jésu-way and later go to the Heaven place."

I feel confused. "Can you call on Jésu with the Black-robe touching sign?" I move my hand from my head to my chest and to each shoulder, mimicking what I had seen the followers of Old Ignácio do. "Is it like when Salish people point the pipe in the four directions before smoking?"

He smiles his one-sided smile. "There is not much that your eyes do not see." He makes the crossing sign. "Jésu is always here...his spirit, that is. The touching sign is just a reminder. So you will not be afraid."

How nice to be never afraid. I finger the empty leather amulet around my neck. Soon I will fill it with objects from my own spirit-partner quest after I become a woman. Will its medicine help me not be afraid?

I stoke Shy Bird's neck. "Can Jésu help me become a horse healer?"

"Jésu can help you be a good person," he says. "I can help you become a horse healer. And a horse rider."

The sense that I can trust this man grows inside me. I ask, "Will you help me? If I come here when you are guarding the herd, when you have the watch, can you teach me about the horses without anyone knowing?"

His reply is long in coming. "It is not good to keep things under blanket, but your guiding spirit is strong. I will pray on this. If it is the will of Jésu, I will help."

That marks the beginning of our pact. Through four seasons of my tenth winter and four of the next, I become Stays-With-Horses Girl. To So-chee it is a poking-fun name, but to me and to Snow-Cave Man, it is a good name. I come to the horse meadow at night, after sun-sleep or before sun-awake, to learn about horses, their needs, their habits. Moving from sorrel to pinto to bay to chestnut, I learn to see weakness, hurts or sickness. I become a small shadow to Snow-Cave Man. He teaches me the remedies for colic, sores from riding cinches, wounds, coughing and other illnesses. He teaches me the secret rituals and herbal cures of the horse-healer-way. I let myself imagine how my reputation as a horse healer will spread, and people will seek my help and pay me with horses.

I also learn the horse-riding-way. I become so at one with horse-thought that horse and I are glued together as if with pine resin, knowing each other's needs, wishes, responding to each other's signals, hand on neck, knee on side, heel in ribs, soft nose in hand, breathing together, hair and mane blowing in wind, moon reflecting off skin and hide. I learn how to ask horses to let me sit up on their backs, guide them with my hands, my legs, my voice. Mostly I work with horses that belong to Snow-Cave Man. But sometimes I ride one of Father's horses. Especially Shy Bird, my favorite.

At first, I try to keep my horse visits under the blanket. At night I stuff my sleeping robe with bundles to look like girl asleep. I clean my skin of horse smells with river washing before returning to the lodge I share with Aunt, So-chee and two younger sisters. I continue my half-hearted work at woman-way learning.

But Aunt begins noticing when I fall asleep during suntime. She asks about the reddish patches on my legs and ankles from rubbing on horse hide. One night she discovers the lumps in my sleeping blankets are not me. I tell her that sleep sometimes does not come for me and I go for walks. I convince her at first, but her suspicion is growing.

I mind-journey to a night when the half-moon is lowering toward the mountains, soon to be sun-awake time. It is the Moon of Full Leaves, when sunlight lasts long, and warmth lingers into the night. Shy Bird greets me with a soft nicker. She sniffs my hair as I rub her withers. I take a long breath and feel a deep comfort in my heart.

I untie the picket rope, grasp her mane and swing onto her back. No leather rein is looped around the horse's lower jaw, no blanket, no saddle. Thigh pressure, leg squeezing, weight shifting, hands guiding—these are my asking-way.

Holding her mane in both hands, I lean over her neck and urge her into a lope, then a gallop. Aaah, how she runs! Flying! Her mane mixes with my hair. Our hearts pound as one. I bring her to a skidding stop in a shower of dirt and pebbles, swing her to left and right on her hind legs, back her up, cross-step her sideways.

Finally I dismount, re-tie the picket rope, and wipe the mare clean with a square of tanned hide. I say goodbye to Shy Bird and start back to Aunt's lodge before the still hidden sun paints the western mountain tops with bright orange. I hear her nicker again as I leave.

Snow-Cave-Man steps out from the shadows at the edge of the horse meadow. He limps over to greet me. His lop-sided smile flashes in the moonlight. "You are becoming quite a night rider."

A part of me is smiling. Another part feels heavy. "I wish Father would.... I wish it didn't always have to be at night."

"Jésu will show you a way to your spirit path."

I hope he is right. My mind seeks a way to make him right.

A clicking sound brings me back to now-time on red-cliff ridge. I twist around to see if Lena's spirit-being is showing itself again from behind that big juniper upslope. All see is a deer. An old buck, big, with five tips on each antler, two of them broken. He stares at me with eyes that seem to want something. It reminds me of someone or some happening I cannot place. It walks toward me a few steps, and I notice it is limping. It lowers its head, sniffs, catches my scent, backs away without breaking its gaze.

My eyelids grow heavy. I lay my blanket on the hard ground and lie down to sleep for a while. Maybe Lena will come to me in a dream.

7

SNOW-CAVE MAN

Snow-Cave Man gazes at Takánsy's still form, cushioned by a blanket on the flat sandstones on the edge-world between the Land of Living and the Great Beyond. He flicks his huge ears at her, catches the slow rhythm of her sleep breathing. She is close to cross-over. She may be able to hear him. At this stage, some can, some cannot. He will try after she awakens. He shakes his antlers and turns to leave. Once behind the juniper, he walks to the edge of the red cliff, steps off into empty space and shape-shifts into human form. He is fifty winters again, not the shriveled wreck of a man he was when he died. He walks among the glowing creatures and people of the spirit world he calls Heaven, sits down on a moss-covered stump to think, and remember.

He time-journeys back to the Bitterroot meadow where his and Ironhand's horses graze in the time before the Black-robe coming.

Takánsy has ten winters of age and is just starting her journey from girl to horse woman of high standing. He likes this girl, her spirited pursuit of horse wisdom, her love of the four-legged ones. Her father loves the wealth that his horses create; she loves them for themselves because she connects with their inner spirits.

Takánsy is standing with him beside Shy Bird. Suddenly voices rise from the place where the path from the village enters the horse meadow. The girl tenses, moves away from the black mare. Ironhand steps into the clearing, followed by her brother, Little Bear. They walk toward Snow-Cave Man through the grass, faces flushed, arms waving, energy sparking between them. Horses' heads rise, ears point forward, teeth stop chewing.

Ironhand's right leg drags through the grass. His left hand punches the air, his face intent as a wolf on the hunt. Little Bear, looking like he wishes he could hide from that wolf, holds a blanket and leather loop rein in his arms.

As they draw closer, Ironhand's gaze skips over Takánsy and fixes on Snow-Cave Man. Not bothering with the customary greeting, he barks out a question.

"What report do you have on the horses?" His voice is raspy, impatient.

Snow-Cave-Man forces his face into a smile. With a nod he says, "God be with thee. Greetings to Ironhand and Little Bear." He pauses for a reply. Receiving none, he says, "The horses are all fine except for that Palomino. Your daughter says he has the shin soreness."

Ironhand's eyebrows bunch into a frown as he glances at Takánsy before returning his gaze to Snow-Cave Man. "And what say you?"

"It is true." Snow-Cave Man resists the urge to look at Takánsy, who, he senses, has taken a step backward.

Ironhand's frown darkens as he turns to Little Bear. "Will you not learn?" He snatches the blanket out of his son's hand, limps over to a large bay gelding picketed a few paces away, and tosses the blanket over the bay's back. "This bay better not develop shin soreness." He settles the blanket into place and secures it with a strip of leather tied around the horse's mid-section, just behind the front legs.

Little Bear's face remains blank as stone, but Snow-Cave Man can feel the anger flow out toward Takánsy, a trickle threatening to become a flood. Little Bear is a thin copy of his father, not as tall, but with the same tall forehead and narrow nose. He is separated from Takánsy by four winters of age and by the gulf that separates all young warriors-in-training from their younger sisters.

Little Bear slips a leather loop rein over the horse's lower jaw and swings onto its back. The bay steps nervously to the side. Little Bear presses his legs together and urges the big horse forward.

"Walk him out first," Ironhand says. "His

power is strong and he wants to use it up at the beginning. Little Bear must learn to control him."

Little Bear tries to ease the gelding into a walk but the horse prances sideways and jerks his head, crow-hopping in eagerness to be off. The young warrior jerks on the bay's rein. Face flushing, he darts a glance at his father and is met with an arrow stare.

"That bay will run well at the next Camas-root Moon race," Snow-Cave-Man says, attempting to ease the boy's discomfort. "The Pend d'Oreilles will be in for a surprise."

Ironhand's eyes never leave the bay and Little Bear, but he smiles, revealing another casualty of his fight with the Blackfeet: a missing front dog-tooth.

"Yes. Let's hope they place big bets."

"And your son is light in weight and strong in arm, a good combination. You have trained him well."

Ironhand makes no response. He walks toward Little Bear and says, "Go. Show me what you can do."

Little Bear digs in his heels and the gelding leaps forward. Clods fly and hooves thud on the meadow turf as they tear around the edge of the pasture. Shy Bird calls out in an excited whinny, and several other horses dance around straining at their tethers.

Snow-Cave Man turns to Takánsy. "That horse is fast."

Takánsy's eyes gleam as she watches the bay race to the edge of the clearing and turn, settling into a more even pace.

Voice guarded, she whispers, "Fast for a short run. But see how he slows now? My brother needs to talk to that horse, save some energy for the end."

Snow-Cave Man studies her face. Lips parted, gray eyes intent, her body rocks ever so slightly in rhythm with the big horse's stride. He realizes she is imagining herself in the place of Little Bear.

Finishing the circuit, Little Bear rides back to his father and dismounts. Ironhand, eyes narrowed, begins talking racing strategy, hands punching the air.

Snow-Cave Man sighs. He depends on Ironhand for much of the food he needs. Hunting has been difficult for him since his vision quest on Shining Mountain. In return, he guards the great man's horse herd--and keeps quiet about his dislike for Ironhand's bragging-way, how he uses his warrior reputation for his own gain, hiding his true purposes under a blanket.

Snow-Cave Man glances down at his missing toes. They block him from the warrior path, as does his belief in Jésu. These things set him on a path apart from the people. Not that he is shunned or treated with disrespect. But sometimes he feels like a crippled deer left behind by the herd. And toes are not his only missing parts. His own capacity for fatherhood was severed during a knife fight with a rival when he was staying with the Iroquois people. It was why he left that tribe to return to his Salish band. It was why he has never taken wives. About this he has never spoken to anyone except Jésu. His solace and hope rest in the Black-robe religion, which sets him apart from others.

A little like her, he thinks, glancing at Takánsy.

The girl is still fixated on her father's teaching. She whispers, as much to herself as to him, "How can I show Father I can ride too, that

I am worthy of his training?" Without waiting for an answer, she steps forward to stand beside her father. Snow-Cave Man follows.

She tugs at the buckskin fringe on Ironhand's sleeve.

Her father glances down, eyes narrowing. "What?"

"Father, will you teach me the racing-way?"

"No." He turns back to Little Bear.

She stiffens, hesitates, then reaches out for another fringe tug. "But Father, I can ride. Please, let me show you."

He twists around, face bowstring taut. "Quiet! I am trying to train your brother."

"But can't I be trained too? I can listen to..."

"STOP IT!" Arrows fly from his eyes.

She cowers back, stumbling into Snow-cave Man.

"Stay away from these horses!" Ironhand steps forward, fist shaking. "Look at you. No beadwork, no braids. You look like a poor man's daughter. No young man will offer me a decent bride price if you can't even..." He pauses to catch his breath and lowers his voice a little. "Your mother says you do not listen to her teaching. Go to her at once. Go!"

Takánsy turns and hurries past Snow-Cave Man toward the path to the village. "She is not my mother," he hears her mutter as she passes.

Head held high, she tries not to run, but breaks into a trot and swipes her eyes with the back of her hands just before she disappears into the willow bushes.

Snow-Cave-Man watches her retreat, wondering if she will return to the horse meadow.

Three nights later she does. As she grooms Shy Bird, he ventures the thought that her father's teaching-way may be hurting rather than helping her brother.

To his surprise, she turns on him, eyes fierce.

"My father is a great teacher, as he is a great warrior. I have heart-pride in him. It is all Little Bear's fault he does not learn." She leads Shy Bird to a stump, steps up and swings herself onto the horse's back. Using only her hands, legs and voice, she lopes across the meadow into the moonlit darkness.

8

TRIAL QUEST

I come awake. The stone on which I sit is cutting into my rump. How long have I been asleep? I glance up and see that Sun has not traveled much further in its sky journey. I look around the red-cliff ridge. No sign of Lena's spirit. Have I been foolish trying to reach her?

I push myself to my feet. I look down slope to the grove of piñons where my horse is usually tied, along with my parfleche bag. Nothing there. How, I wonder, have I come to this place?

I walk back upslope to the big juniper where Lena's spirit-being appeared. The old buck with the broken antlers stands a few paces further on, flicking its big ears at me. I pause, sit and rest my back against the tree. The deer's old, faded eyes seem to brighten, searching mine. One side of its muzzle lifts slightly in what appears to be a lop-sided grin.

I stare, astonished. "Snow-Cave Man?"

The buck bobs its head as if agreeing. Or maybe it is just shaking off a fly. I resist the urge to run toward it.

I ask, "Do you know where my Lena is?"

The old buck shows no sign of understanding.

I ask again, more urgently.

The buck looks away, browses on a bush.

I sigh, lean my head back against the tree. The deer limps away.

I think about my girlhood quest for a horse spirit-partner. How I gained its medicine, then lost it due to my mistakes. Mistakes that started before my moon-time, when I was doing practice quests.

Lena would not understand about such things. Here at the Crossing, Lightfaces believe spirit-partners are foolish superstitions. Medina would never agree to send his daughter off to spend nights alone with no food, and as follower of the Black-robe-way, I did not push on her a quest. Besides, Lena already had a connection to the horse-spirit. No quest needed. Her spirit path and mine, the same.

Now I feel heart-heavy about Lena's no-quest. Jésu did not give her the protection. Maybe with a Salish spirit-partner she would have been protected. Would have escaped her cross-over journey.

I shake my head to cast off this useless thought. It will not bring her back.

I mind-journey back to my first all-night trial quest when I have twelve winters of age. An afternoon near the end of the Greening Moon, when the Weather Spirit cannot decide between winter or spring. Aunt tells me it is time.

"Your coming-of-age is near, and you must practice being out alone at night. You must prepare your body and mind for the many-day quest after your first moon-time when you become a woman."

I look at my chest. No buds yet. But Aunt, she is right. Time to prepare.

Unlike other girls, I look forward to an all-night vigil. My age-mates pretend to be brave about this, but their eyes grow big at the thought of a night alone, away from lodge-safety. Maybe this is something I can do better than they, I think.

Before, when I had only six winters, Aunt sent me on my first trial quest. Not overnight, just an easy trip to the river at dusk to fetch a small skin of water. I was singing, happy while returning to Aunt's lodge, not afraid.

Next Aunt sent me into the dark spruce woods to bring some kinnikinic leaves for tea. A bear came sniffing along, upwind from me, hunting grubs. I stood very still. The bear didn't smell me, and I was not afraid.

By my twelfth winter the trial quests got longer and more difficult, often bringing me home in the dark. That's what trial quests are supposed to do, help you get used to being alone and in the dark. I did not need such help. The night was already my friend, guardian of my horse visits.

Now, at twelve winters of age, it is time for my first all-night practice quest. Aunt sends me to a small meadow next to a place named Big Pine, a short distance from our new village, a sun-to-middle-of-sky ride upstream on the Bitterroot, where we have moved to give our horses new grass. She tells me to sit next to the pine until Moon passes across the sky and darkness comes. She tells me to not return to the lodge until after first light.

Aunt's hands flutter first to her cheeks, then her mouth, then to her lap, like frightened sparrows.

She says, "While you sit there, be very quiet and watch everything that happens—especially the animals you see, or anything unusual. Remember these things and tell me about them in the morning."

I smile, take up my sleeping mat, a water skin and some pemmican to eat.

"No food," Aunt says. "The spirits will not come if you eat. On your woman's quest, how will you get through ten nights without food if you do not practice now?"

I want to ignore her, but think of Father's arrow eyes. My pemmican stays with Aunt.

I set out after Sun dips behind the Bitterroot mountains. Long shadows of fir trees reach toward me until darkening purple sky turns into night. Meadow grass swishes against my legs. The smell of green. I hum a soft tune. A gray jay, settling on its pine perch for the night, cocks its head and cries *chuck, chuck, wheeooo*—night, night, welcome.

In Big Pine meadow, I find a swirled depression in the grass—a deer lie. Here I sit next to the pine tree and wait. Crickets chirp beside a marshy spot. Small creatures rustle in the grass. Whispers stir the leaves in trees around the meadow. Smells of damp earth and greening leaves. But I see nothing, not even a mouse or a vole. I doze for a while, then more waiting. Nothing. Too much nothing.

I stand and begin pacing around the clearing, wondering why no animals are visiting me. Then I think, If I want to see a horse-spirit, why not go where horses are? In the pasture there are no lookouts posted during the greening moon, a time when Blackfeet raiders are not expected because they are hunting buffalo on the plains to end the winter hunger time. No one will see me.

Breaking rules. Disobeying Aunt. Disobeying Father. No one will know. Such a little thing, it won't matter, I tell myself

At the morning meal I tell Aunt I saw a gray jay.

"Is that all?" she asks.

I tell her, yes. I tell her the bird flew from the big pine to my sitting place. That it hopped close to me, cocking its head, in dark, after roosting time. Strange, I say. Maybe a sign. Maybe my spirit-partner.

Aunt smiles, satisfied with my forked-tongue story. About the horses I speak no word. I begin my practice quests with the lying-way. As time passes I get better and better at telling forked-tongue stories.

I make a vow to obey Aunt on my next trial quest. Resist the call of the horse meadow. Stay alone in Big Pine Meadow, no food, sitting still, waiting for horse-spirit to come.

But when the next trial quest comes, I skip the spirit waiting and go directly to the horses. The lure of night riding is stronger than the quest for spirit connection. My stays-with-horses feeling, so strong, like moth-drawn-to-fire. I wonder if it is right to follow this path.

9

LITTLE BEAR

I time-journey back to another childhood moment with Snow-Cave Man. Four seasons have passed. It is late in the Service Berry moon, when I have twelve winters behind me. Berries are ripening, leaves starting to turn. The people are preparing to leave for the winter buffalo hunt on the three rivers plain, far toward sun-awake.

I fox-walk down to the horse meadow to where Father is training my brother, Little Bear, in the racing-way. From behind a bush at meadow's edge I watch Father's eagle focus on my brother. He does not notice me, even when looking in my direction, even when I sneeze. What would it be like, I wonder, to hold his attention like that, to count for something big in his eyes? A thought part thrill, part danger.

Little Bear is becoming a good rider. But he rides the big bay always commanding, never asking. Never taking time to find out if his horse feels well or is distracted or hungry. He thinks about himself, how he is seen by Father's eyes, and so never gets the most out his horse.

Watching the bay, I learn that timing is everything. Knowing exactly when to release his full spirit. The exact moment when the remaining distance to the finish line is a match for his last burst of speed.

Shy Bird is different. She is fast, but nervous as a hunted deer, liable to spook at any waving blanket or strange rock in the path. Shy Bird needs a calm rider. And experience to withstand the crowding and confusion of a race start. I can teach her, I think from my hiding place. *But how will I get the chance?*

In my mind-dreams about the next race, I fly first across the finish line on Shy Bird. People erupt in happy-shouts. Father looks at me with proud eyes and glad heart. If only I can find a way to show him how I ride, get him to show me more about the racing-way!

With heavy feet I walk back up the trail to Aunt's lodge. For the rest of the afternoon I work to finish beading a small buckskin pouch for Father. Later that night I give it to him to wear on his belt for good luck medicine.

He is preparing his pipe, so he sets my gift on his crippled knee and grunts. Three sleeps later

I find it in the trash midden. I do not feel angry at this. My beadwork is bad, not deserving of his notice. I need other ways to gain his favor.

Another winter passes, my thirteenth. Early in the Greening Moon, winter chill still in the air, I notice that Father's big bay racing horse is coughing. He is picketed outside First Wife's lodge, along with two buffalo runner horses. These three are now too valuable to be left with other horses in night pasture. It is Little Bear's job to bring these special horses back to the lodge as the sky darkens, check their feet, brush and trim their manes and feed them.

The bay's cough is not rib-shaking, but still a cause for worry. He must be in good condition for upcoming horse races. I wonder what might be causing it. Behind First Wife's lodge I find the answer. Old grass and cottonwood inner bark from last fall piled under a bush, mostly hidden, some gray with mold. Its musty scent invades my nose. Little Bear is being lazy. Instead of hauling fresh cut grass from meadows along the river, he is feeding the horse with something easier to get. The bay will be weakened on this kind of food. Father must be told.

I find Father at the lodge of Big Face, our chief, near the center of the circle of lodges. Big Face is the only one with bigger lodge than Father's. They are talking about the Camas-root Moon race, when our people will join the Pend Orielle people at the camas meadows for the annual feast and root ceremony. At this time bets will be wagered and races run. The very race Little Bear is being trained for.

When the talking is finished, I step in beside Father to get him to notice me, dodging his walking stick as he hurries along. I tell him about the bay horse's cough and grab his hand to lead him to the moldy grass. At the sight of it, his face thunderclouds and his eyes lightning-spark. For once, the bolts are not aiming at me. He stalks away, leaving me standing there wondering what will happen. Worrying whether I have done a good thing.

Later that afternoon in Aunt's lodge, Little Bear does not come to supper. At night when sister So-chee and I are starting to doze in our buffalo sleeping robes, the lodge flap opens and in he comes. He is rubbing a spot on his leg, and even in the darkness I see that his right eye is swollen shut. He comes over and squats beside me. I keep my eyes closed, trying to make the sleep breathing sound.

His hissed words make me want to crawl into a hole.

"Whore bitch. You will pay."

The cold that seizes my heart is worse than the cold air that blows in from the lodge flap as he leaves. I lie there staring at the smoke hole in the top of the lodge. Sleep is slow in coming.

Someone's toe pushing against my leg nudges me awake.

"You look like you have been wrestling with Spirits all night." So-chee reaches down and slaps a tuft of meadow grass from my hair. "Come on, Aunt is waiting. You are holding up the root gathering trip."

I rise, pull on my moccasins, wrap myself in a blanket and step outside.

Little Bear is standing there. "Go without her." he growls to So-chee.

I jump back. Shielding my eyes, I see him smacking his lips as he chews a chunk of trout meat stripped from a backbone with a long white row of needle-thin ribs.

"Father has something to tell her." There is a gleam in his half-shut eye.

So-chee puts on her best goading smile. "Why? Is Father going to let her ride the Bay instead of you?"

Our brother's face holds steady. But the fish backbone snaps in his hand, and his voice sounds thin as a bowstring about to break. "Spoken by one who cannot tell horse from elk." He rises, points a finger at me and tells me to go to First Wife's lodge, where Father waits. He stalks away.

I clutch the blanket around my shoulders and make my way to the opening in the big lodge, flanked by painted black hands on the buffalo-hide cover. Father is sitting against his back rest at the rear, licking the remains of stewed venison from his fingers. First Wife is not in sight. He waves me in through the lodge flap and gives me a hard stare. My gaze fixes on the ground. My knees are shaking.

"You are going to the horses at night, riding that black mare." It is not a question. His voice is calm, not thunder.

I risk a glance at him. Stern face, but no arrow eyes. Someone must have seen me riding and told him. I wonder what my punishment will be.

"You are soon a woman, yet you do not keep to the woman's path."

"Father, I..."

He cuts me off. "When you come of age, you must be ready. What young man will bring me gifts to wed a woman who cannot bead and sew and cook and tan hides? Look at you. You are ugly. No meat on your bones. Strange eyes that shrivel a man's pole. What value are you without the woman skills?"

"Father, I will be ready, I promise."

"Promises. Ha! I must hear of this from Aunt. And soon. Now go!" He picks up a rib bone and throws it at me. It thuds against my chest. I duck down and back out of the lodge.

Face hot, I return to Aunt's lodge, thinking I must do as he says. But I am also thinking, he does not forbid me from riding! And another thought is burrowing into my mind, luring me toward an action as thrilling as it is dangerous.

10

HARD WINTER

From behind a thicket of wild plum on the red-cliff ridge, Snow-Cave Man watches Takánsy struggle with her memories. Eyes closed, lost in thought, her age-spotted hands twitch from time to time as she reaches back to re-live her past. As he listens to her thoughts, he wishes he could help her, but the time is not yet ripe. He does not know where her daughter is. He does not know whether Takánsy's thoughts are reaching her like they reach him. He will bide his time. He has plenty to spare. He has already helped several spirit-beings cross over into the next world. He will search his memory for clues about how he might help her. Maybe he will remember something important, some memory holes to fill in.

He mind-journeys back to the time of Takánsy's thirteenth winter, the winter of the long freeze, as the people recorded it on their winter-count skins.

Frigid air thickens the ice on all but the fastest moving river water, making it hard to catch fish. Game is scarce. Hunger gnaws at shrunken stomachs. The sleeves on Takánsy's shirt fall loose around her thinning arms. His own legs are almost as thin as his wooden walking stick.

The winter buffalo hunt turns out badly. Out on the plains to the sun-awake side of the mountains where much of the tribe spends two moons hunting, killing, skinning and carving up buffalo to bring back to the Bitterroot, Blackfeet raiders kill a dozen warriors and kidnap three women, including one of the wives of Two-Scalps, the hunt chief. People return early to their homeland with barely half the usual meat supply.

He tells Takánsy that Blackfeet warriors are not better fighters than Salish warriors, that he believes they are lazy and more cowardly. But they have one big advantage: black powder weapons. They get them from the Lightskins who live further toward sun-awake, trading guns for beaver pelts and buffalo robes. And with their weapon advantage, the Blackfeet are ruthless in driving other people out of the three rivers country where the big buffalo herds live.

As he listens to campfire councils, wrapped in his trade blanket against the freezing cold,

Snow-Cave Man hears hunters talk of failed spirit-partners and sees worry-frowns on their brows. Two-Scalps grumbles that the pre-hunt dancing, praying and shaman conjuring no longer seems to help. He wonders aloud: "Is Amotken abandoning the people? Is their medicine leaving them?"

Fear and defeat are driving people to look for new spirit paths, just as hunger drives people to eat their horses.

Old Ignácio, the Iroquois, urges adopting the Black-robe religion. He tells of the great medicine of Jésu, of how villages with Jesuit priests prosper, how their cures protect people from the red-spot disease, how warriors using the Catholic touching sign defeat their enemies. As if to prove him right, two of the most successful of the Salish hunters are followers of Old Ignácio.

Those followers are growing in number. When Snow-Cave Man attends seventh day song and prayer gatherings, there are now too many people to fit inside Old Ignácio's lodge, or even four of such lodges. Among them, to Snow-Cave Man's surprise, is Chief Big Face himself. He comes with two of his wives and four of his sons. He reminds his people of the legend of Shining Shirt, the ancient, white-haired Salish shaman from the long ago, who prophesied the arrival of Lightskins before the visit of Lewis and Clark. His vision also foretold the arrival of medicine men in long black robes whose *sumesh* is great.

Snow-Cave Man likes Old Ignácio. Appreciates his modesty. The Iroquois does not use his position to strut his power or gather wealth. Although he leads songs and prayers, and tells stories of "saints," he refuses to recite the Jésu prayer. Says he is not qualified. Only a Jésuit priest, a Black-robe, can do that. Only a Black-robe, he says, can read out of the mysterious holy book with black marks on thin leaf pages that impart powerful medicine.

Snow-Cave Man remembers how in the previous spring, Old Ignácio and several other men left the Bitterroot to visit Black-robe priests in a place called Saint Louis, far toward sun-awake. But when they asked for a priest to return with him to the Bitterroot, the Black-robes turned him down. Not enough priests to send, they said.

When Old Ignácio returned, he told stories about the Lightskins that caused people's eyes to widen. So many Lightskins, more than can be counted, with lodges made from stone and wood, and huge, white winged canoes on vast rivers delivering all manner of marvelous trade goods. Powerful medicine indeed!

Now, after the harsh winter, sentiment is growing for another attempt to bring back a Black-robe. Chief Bigface asks Old Ignácio to make another journey. The Iroquois agrees, smiling a huge smile. He plans to set off for Saint Louis after next winter's snow melt.

Snow-Cave Man prays for the success of such a journey. He would go himself if it were not for his crippled toes. In the meantime, he offers his encouragement to curious members of the Salish band by telling them of his beliefs. He never tries to persuade. Only offers his own story when asked. People gather to hear about his escape from freezing death in the snow cave on Shining Mountain. They shiver as they listen.

Some of them tell Snow-Cave Man they wish to walk the Black-robe-way. He does not always welcome this. Their purpose is often gaining wealth, victory over enemies, or protection from disease. In his experience, Jésu does not stop bad things from happening or cause good things upon request. His own prayers to Jésu had not saved his parents from the red-spot sickness. They died shortly after his return from the Iroquois, a blow that fell right after his own loss of manhood, his own hope for a future family. But Jésu had comforted him through this spirit-crushing ordeal, helped him mend the tear in his heart. How this happened is hard to explain to himself, let alone others, so he does not try.

Nor does he want to add to the rumbles of division between Black-robe followers and those who follow traditional ways. Old Crazy Bones, the shaman, shakes his rattles and warns anyone who will listen to reject the Lightskin road. Some of the warriors agree with him. Some of them, like Ironhand, openly mock Old Ignácio and his hymn-singing meetings.

For the most part, Salish people are tolerant of others' beliefs. Respectful of each other's spirit-partner choices, which are considered private matters, seldom talked about. Snow-Cave Man wants to keep it that way. It is hard enough to fight Blackfeet raiders without fighting among themselves.

In this, Snow-Cave Man finds an ally in Otter Woman. She is a highly respected medicine-woman, famous for her collection of medicine herbs and knowledge of how to use them. An elder with seventy winters, with a wrinkled face enlivened by shrewd eyes, she engages him in talk about his Jésu beliefs.

Her father and mother are also dead, felled by the same red-spot sickness that took his parents. Her three husbands and two children are also lost, not to sickness, but to Blackfeet attacks, horse accidents and drowning. Bonded in tragedy, she and Snow-Cave Man sometimes talk long into the night about the mysteries of medicine and the afterlife of the spirit world.

"Why do Black-robes claim powerful medicine for a young man who got himself tortured and hung up to die on a tree?" she asks.

He counters, "Jésu's life returned after three sleeps. Is this not big *sumesh*?"

"What about this strange mind-thought of 'sin?'" she wonders. "Leading to an afterlife in the burning Hell place? In the Salish Great Beyond, spirit-beings lead the same kind of life as here, with bad people eventually getting there once they cross the chasm after four seasons of trials."

He replies, "This is something neither of us will know until after our own cross-over journeys."

She winks and smiles. "On that we agree."

He asks, "What about your own spirit-partner, the otter? Do you really believe an animal spirit is the source of your healing *sumesh*?"

With a sly grin, she replies, "My herbs do the work. The otter *sumesh* helps people believe they will work."

And so on. Snow-Cave Man grows to treasure these talks. Better than the loneliness of his empty lodge during the long winter nights.

On the coldest times during the winter of the long freeze, Snow-Cave Man is sometimes invited into Takánsy's Aunt's lodge to warm himself and share a late afternoon meal. He is grateful for this kindness. He likes hearing children's laughter and women's soothing chatter. Although he has grown used to being alone, the memory of his own mother's crooning voice, his father's gruff assurances, sometimes leave him with a hole in his heart.

Here in Aunt's lodge he watches Takánsy work on her woman's-way skills. Her beadwork is improving, he sees, not like So-Chee's, but acceptable. She carries wood, cleans, cooks, sews—everything Aunt asks her to do. She is mostly quiet, but steals glances at him whenever the talk turns to horses. Although she is thin, she does not fall ill.

Neither do the horses that she and he care for. To keep the horses' ribs from showing under their winter hair, he and Takánsy cut and haul dried grass and inner cottonwood bark to the meadow. Shy Bird makes it through the winter pretty well. So do Ironhand's mounts, except for two old mares that are close to their crossover time anyway and are killed for food. Other people's horses are not so lucky. When sun-times grow longer and the first hopeful shoots of green begin poking up through the warming earth, there are fewer horses to enjoy the coming forage. Their sacrifices sustain many people through the winter. Snow-Cave Man thanks Jésu for their deliverance.

As nights grow warmer, Takánsy again takes up her night riding. Snow-Cave Man watches as his Stays-With-Horses girl and Shy Bird grow so attuned to each other that mere wishes become actions. He marvels how they move as a single being. He senses a tiny seed sprouting in the girl's mind, growing and spreading like nettles along the riverbank. She never speaks of it, but he sees how she gazes into the distance, mind lost in dream-thought.

When he asks her what she is thinking, she answers with "nothing" or "just listening to bird calls."

Not until the Camas-root Moon race does he discover the secret of her dream-thought.

11

THE RACE

I rouse myself from my juniper tree backrest on the red-cliff ridge. My mind journeys back to the Camas-root Moon race after the winter of the long freeze. The memory of that race brings me struggling to my feet and pacing in a tight circle, breathing hard.

People begin preparations for The Camas-root Moon festival after winter, when daylight lengthens and new grass springs from warming soil. Like everyone else, I am eager to celebrate the brief blooming season when the camas roots are the most succulent and everyone is hungry for something besides our diminishing winter food supplies.

The Pend d'Oreilles people, our Salish relatives from cold-ward, will join us for feasting, dancing, games, gambling, and a First Roots ceremony. Young men and women will eye each other under the watchful gaze of elders. And toward the end there will be horse-racing. That is what quickens my heartbeat.

When the chief gives the signal, we break down our lodges, pack our belongings, load our horses and depart for the beautiful meadow toward the mouth of the Bitterroot River where the gathering takes place. When we arrive, I help Aunt set up our lodge on the sun-asleep side of the circle of lodges.

Snow-Cave Man sets his up next to us.

When everyone is settled in, Chief Big Face appoints two women to gather First Roots. One is the wife of Old Ignácio. The other is Ironhand's First Wife. As Ironhand escorts First Wife to the edge of the boggy area blooming with blue camas flowers, I feel heart-pride.

"A great honor," I say to Snow-Cave Man.

"Wise," Snow-Cave Man replies. "One woman is a Black-robe follower, the other walks the spirit path road. Good balance."

The two women walk barefoot into the bog. The sun is bright, the sky cloudless cobalt blue. First Wife raises her arms and prays to Amotken for the people's health, safety, and hunting success. Then she prays to the earth, Mother of plants, for an abundant root harvest.

Old Ignácio's wife folds her hands and offers a Jésu prayer and a hymn-song followed by the crossing sign.

Then they begin to dig.

When their baskets are full, they bring them to the Chief's lodge and place the roots in the rock-lined cooking pit, where they roast for the next three sleeps. Then the wives of Big Face prepare the camas roots for distribution to all the people for the ceremonial first bite.

Chief Big Face points his lance first to the sun, then to the earth, praying to each. He steps away from the steaming pit after making the crossing sign over it. Sweet-smelling steam drifts through our circle of onlookers. My mouth waters.

Women come forward to take a few roots back to their families. No one is allowed to harvest their own roots until this ritual is complete. Ironhand's First Wife brings roots to So-Chee and Little Bear and the other wives and children that make up Ironhand's four lodges. She barely has enough to give to Aunt, who breaks off a small taste for me. Snow-Cave Man receives nothing. He swallows and waits for the bigger meal to come.

Two sleeps later, the time for horse racing comes. Sun is beaming, wind is still, but the chill morning air raises bumps on my skin as people gather at the racing meadow.

Women wear bright blue camas flowers in their braided hair. Their pinched winter faces have filled out, their energy restored. Men's faces are painted, each with his own design, each wearing his finest clothes bedecked with quills, beads and feathers. Two scantily clad little boys crying "hai,

hai," pop suddenly out of a lodge opening and charge off astride sticks, shoving each other to gain the lead.

Snow-Cave Man wears his usual plain buckskin pants and shirt. Like other Black-robe followers, he wears no face paint. I join him to walk to the racing meadow. He notices the new beadwork on my buckskin sleeves—black beads sewn in the shape of a black hand with fingers pointing up.

"My father's sign," I explain.

We reach the giant boulders marking the start of the racing meadow. From there, the racing pathway runs straight for a hundred paces, curves around a tall pine at the end of the meadow, continues up a little hill with a large gray boulder on top, then swings back down a long slope to the starting place. Two boys stretch a rope between the two boulders. A Pend d'Oreille man rolls a large drum into place near one of the boulders. All is ready.

My eyes rove over the racing meadow to fix each swale, turn and tuft of grass in my mind. Snow-Cave Man leans toward me to explain how the riders must stay outside of the tree and far boulder to qualify. I tell him I have already walked the race path three times. He shoots me a questioning look. I turn away, not wanting to reveal my dream-thoughts of racing Shy Bird.

Nearby, riders hold their racehorses next to a roped off area where men are haggling over their bets. Ears on alert, necks arched, the animals paw the ground, snort and side-step. I imagine Shy Bird among them, ready to race with me on her back. But she is behind Snow-Cave Man's lodge where I picketed her that morning.

The men gather in small clumps to ply

each other for information about the horses and riders. In the center of one cluster, I see Father, cheeks painted with black triangles pointing down to highlight his arrow eyes. I feel a surge of pride. He stands face-to-face with a stout Pend d'Oreille man.

Raising his hand, Father says, "The stallion of my Pend d'Oreille friend looks nervous."

All eyes shift to the sorrel horse a few paces away being held by a frowning young man. The stallion paws the ground and snorts.

"He always looks this way before winning a race," the Pend d'Oreille man says. He is short but solid, a tree stump of a man. He stares at Father through hooded eyes, a bristle-backed dog sizing up a rival. "What about your bay gelding over there. Is he favoring that back left leg?"

All eyes shift to where Little Bear stands holding Father's big bay. Like the other riders, my brother is stripped down to his loincloth and moccasins. A stripe of red paint runs from his forehead down between his eyes to the tip of his nose. It is supposed to make him look fierce, but to me, it looks as if he has blundered headlong into a painted pole.

Father shrugs. "It is nothing. Come, we will have a look." He walks over, squeezes the gelding's fetlock and raises its hoof into his cupped hand.

"I think this horse will be ready to run at race time," he says, letting the hoof drop. Little Bear leads the horse away. The gelding steps gingerly on its foot.

No one seems to notice what I see, a small lump on the hoof's underside daubed over with mud.

Betting begins in earnest. Into the roped-off enclosure men place beaver pelts, buffalo robes, guns, knives, trade blankets, and crude little straw figures representing horses. In return, each receives a painted wood stick representing the horse he hopes will win. At the end of the race, the owner of the winning horse will retrieve his own goods and half the goods of the losing side. The rest will be split among those who bet on the winner's horse.

Many sticks representing the Pend d'Oreille's red stallion disappear into eager hands. The Pend d'Oreille man increases his bet on his own stallion by two more horse figures. Father removes a horse figure from his pile. I wonder if he is worried about the bay. I wish I were riding Shy Bird in Little Bear's place.

Little Bear leads the bay behind First Wife's lodge. As soon as he disappears, I run to the lodge and peer cautiously around. Little Bear is holding the bay's hind foot in one hand while prying at the hoof's underside with his knife. A small pebble, no bigger than the tip of his little finger, pops out and rolls into the sand. There is a small knife slit in the under-hoof where the pebble had been inserted.

Shocked, I step forward and blurt, "You are causing that horse to limp."

Little Bear startles. The bay gelding steps sideways, jerking its hoof out of the handhold and clopping it down dangerously close to Little Bear's toes.

"Dog fuck!" Little Bear balls his fist and steps toward me. "You stupid bitch pup, you almost got me stomped on. You hope to be a horse woman, but you are so stupid you blunder around and spook them."

"But the pebble..."

"Forget the gods-cursed pebble! You never saw a pebble!"

He advances on me, brandishing his knife.

His free hand shoots into my chest, knocking me backward. I trip and sit with a whump into the sand.

"Your mouth had better stay closed." The knife waves in front of my face.

I push his hand away and scramble to my feet. "When Father..."

The rhythmic thump of the starting drum sounds through the camp. Little Bear sheaths his knife and seizes the rein hanging from the startled bay's mouth. Still glaring at me, he leads the bay out from behind the lodge, leaps onto its back and wheels away toward the starting area.

Little Bear's rock-in-hoof trick, then his shove, sets me in motion. Anger overcomes my caution. I brush myself off and run to Snow-Cave Man's lodge where Shy Bird is picketed. I leap on her back and follow Little bear to the two boulders.

The drummers raise their beater sticks. At the thump of the drum, the rope drops and the dozen riders launch their mounts between the boulders and onto the racing meadow. They surge toward the first leg of the course toward the tall pine. Shouts erupt from onlookers.

Leaning low over Shy Bird's neck, I gallop between the boulders. She flies over the fallen starting rope without spooking. Ahead of me, clumps of earth and grass fly up from churning hooves. Their thumping sounds grow louder as I gain on the row of heaving horse rumps—black, gray, sorrel, paint—about twenty paces ahead. Gaps appear between faster and slower horses as we near the pine tree at the first turn. I pass two slow horses, a gray and a sorrel.

Ahead, two lead horses round the tree and charge up the hill. The Pend d'Oreille's red stallion and Little Bear's bay gelding are close behind them, running for third place. Seeing Little Bear hunched over the bay's back gives me a kind of target, like aiming an arrow, and Shy Bird, sensing my arrow path, leaps forward past the two trailing racers.

At the pine tree I turn close, forcing the others to the outside. The two lead horses, short-distance sprinters, are beginning to tire. The Pend d'Oreille's red stallion and Little Bear's bay gelding move into the lead. At the crest of the hill, stallion and bay pull away from everyone else.

Everyone except me. My thinness becomes my friend. With lighter weight to carry, Shy Bird flies up the slope like a winged spirit, passing the remaining racers one by one. We round the boulder and start down the gentle slope to the finish. The drumming of stallion and bay hoofbeats replace the sound of the horses lagging behind. The leaders are now only ten paces ahead.

The bodies of Little Bear and the Pend d'Oreille rider curve down like bent bows. They slap leather quirts against their mounts' heaving rumps. The whack of leather on hide mingles with the rasp of labored breathing.

Halfway through the final stretch the red stallion begins to lose ground, slipping backward toward me. I guide Shy Bird away from the flashing quirt, still whapping against the spent animal's red hide. The Pend d'Oreille's mouth flies open as I pass him.

Ahead, Little Bear shouts a victory cry, his mind already at the finish line. He is imagining the cheers of his friends, the inviting glances of young women, the praise from Father. He does not know I am right behind him!

Flecks of foam from the bay gelding's mouth spatter my face. Sweat is strong in my nose. The bay is tiring. Little Bear is saving nothing for the last thirty paces.

Shy Bird's nose draws even with the bay's tail. Little Bear's eyes go round as he twists to look. He cries out a long "Noooooo!" and reins left to cut me off.

Shy Bird veers away but still gains. Her bobbing head draws even with the bay's rump, mid-section, shoulders. We rush toward the finish line between the two boulders. Little Bear turns toward the left boulder, trying to cut me off, but the bay is slowing. With the boulder still twenty paces away, Shy Bird inches ahead.

Sudden as a rattlesnake strike, Little Bear's quirt slashes at my face. The stroke falls short, but Shy Bird, feeling my body flinch, pulls away and rushes directly toward the left boulder. At the last moment, she veers away and flies past the boulder on the outer side. The wrong side. It takes all my strength to stay on her back. She plunges through the scattering crowd and slows to a halt beside Snow-Cave Man's lodge where we began. Shy Bird and I tremble like aspen leaves.

Snow-Cave-Man limps toward me, his smile gone. He reaches out to help me dismount.

"Are you all right?" he asks.

I cling to his hand, my knees shaking. "Yes, only a little..."

"Shaken." He supplies the word. "That was a ride to sing about," he says, finally smiling his one-sided smile. He turns toward Shy Bird. Sweat froths her neck, shoulders and back.

"This horse needs a cooling down walk," he says, slipping a horsehair rope around her neck and leading her away.

I cannot help thinking of her as my horse now. I turn around to see people milling around the other racers as they dismount. I look for Little Bear, but do not see him.

People cluster into groups, one around the roped-off betting area, another around the riders. Some people are coming toward me. I search their faces for a hint of their reaction to my ride.

They crowd around with a drumbeat of questions. "Show us how you guide her without a mouth rein." "How did you overtake the bay?" "What about her training?" I try to answer, surprised at their eager interest. No one seems upset.

But the most important face is not there—Father's. I hear an outburst of angry voices from the betting area. I catch sight of Father, arms waving, hands punching the air, raspy voice rising above the others. Facing him is the Pend d'Oreille man who owns the red stallion.

That is when doubts about the wisdom of my impulse ride start to flood my mind. What, I wonder with growing dread, will Father think?

12

RIVALS

I dart through the circle of curious questioners and run to the roped-off betting enclosure where Father is arguing with the Pend d'Oreille owner of the red stallion. Snow-Cave Man makes his way through the crowd and joins me behind the rope. I ask him about Shy Bird, and he tells me she is behind his lodge, cooled down and well rubbed. Assured, I turn my full attention to what is happening on the other side of the rope.

The Pend d'Oreille man's face flushes a dark shade of red. "That race was no good—the black mare was not supposed to run." His angry tone puts a hush on the crowd. He points to the pile of bets. "I will take mine back." Many of the people who bet against Ironhand nod in agreement. I shake my head in growing alarm.

Father steps in front of the man, blocking his way. A vein bulges in his neck. "There is no rule against other horses running outside the race," he says. "My bay gelding beat your red stallion. The black is also mine. My Pend d'Oreille friend owes Ironhand three horses." A murmur of agreement rises from those few who had cast their lot with Ironhand.

Arguments turn to shouts. A sallow-faced Pend d'Oreille man shoves the shoulder of an uncle of First Wife. Hands reach toward sheathed knives hanging from belts. Snow-Cave Man steps through an opening in the rope, waves his walking stick and shouts, "Let the chiefs decide."

Heads turn, eyes staring. I shrink back, knowing I am to blame for this argument. Snow-Cave Man waves his stick again and repeats his appeal. To my relief, a few voices rise in approval, then grow into agreement. The crowd moves to the lodge of Big Face. Snow-Cave Man hobbles to keep up. I stick close to his side.

Broken Bow, chief of the Pend d'Oreilles, arrives and joins Big Face. Father and the Pend d'Oreilles man argue their cases. The Pend d'Oreilles man steps to one side and crosses his arms to await a decision. Father remains in place. His gaze sweeps the crowd. I edge behind Snow-Cave Man to avoid his eyes. Will Father lose his winnings? That question is a stone in my chest.

The two headmen duck into Big Face's wife's lodge to pass the pipe. The crowd breaks up into twos and threes, some talking quietly, others buzzing with anger. I make myself small and pray that no one will notice me. The scent of tobacco smoke drifts out of the chief's lodge. Finally, the chiefs reappear. People gather back into a semi-circle, faces turned toward the two chiefs. Voices fall silent. Sweat trickles down my sides.

Big Face, the older of the two head men, speaks. "The racing-way custom does not tell us what to do when a surprise horse runs in a race. There is no rule against it. But it does not seem right. We have decided that the losing bettors, those who placed their wagers on the red stallion, may take back one of their bets, the one that is least valuable. That way, they will not lose quite as much. The rest of the bets will be divided as usual among the winners. That way, the winners will still win, but not quite as much as they would if the race had been run as planned."

Murmurs ripple through the onlookers. Most heads nod approval. Ironhand's head stays rigid.

My mouth is dry. Snow-Cave Man turns and pats my shoulder.

The Pend d'Oreille man unfolds his arms and walks over to Ironhand.

"You may claim two of my horses, not three. You may come to my lodge tomorrow to choose." He grunts and turns away.

Father arrow-eyes his rival, then shifts his gaze over the dispersing crowd. His eyes find Snow-Cave Man and me cowering at his side. He pushes toward us, reaches out, grabs my arm and pulls me away.

"After we return to our Bitterroot camp, you will come to First Wife's lodge. We will talk." Father's voice is calm. He turns and limps away.

I am too surprised to reply.

Snow-Cave Man says, "His hand is not lifted in anger?"

I walk with Snow-Cave Man to check on Shy Bird. She nickers at my approach. I rub her back as she nuzzles my neck. My heart calms. Whatever happens, Shy Bird is my storm shelter.

I thank Snow-Cave Man and turn to leave. As I pass the roped-off betting enclosure I see something that sends needles up my spine. Little Bear, lips curled in a silent snarl, black-bead eyes boring into me. I look away and hurry to Aunt's lodge.

The Camas-root Moon festival winds to a close. Some bettors count their winnings while others lament their losses. Women pack up lodges and load their packs with harvested camas roots. New lovers plan future gift exchanges and weddings. The Pend d'Oreilles return to their territory and we to ours. We select a new reach of the Bitterroot where fresh, ungrazed grass awaits our horses. Snow-Cave Man sets up his lodge in a new pasture for his small herd and Father's large one. Father's first wife locates her lodge in the inner circle. As soon as it is set up, I go to meet Father, nervous as a rabbit.

I manage a greeting and Father bids me enter. As my eyes adjust to the dim light, I spot Father against his backrest at the rear of the lodge. For a long time he says nothing, just stares at me. I hug my arms to my chest and look down, unable to hold his gaze. We are alone.

Finally, he says, "I will see more of your horse riding. Not just the black mare, but others, like the big bay. Tomorrow you will come with me and Little Bear to the horse pasture."

He waves me away with a flick of his wrist. I duck out into the sunlight, which seems brighter than when I entered, the shadow of punishment gone. But what will happen tomorrow?

I wake early, pull on my riding clothes and step out of Aunt's lodge into a still-dark morning. Too agitated to eat, I pace around the circle of lodges waiting for Father and Little Bear to emerge. At last they walk out of First Wife's lodge, untie the bay horse and lead it toward the horse meadow. Little Bear walks stiffly, eyes straight ahead, arms held close to his sides. Father spots me and waves me to fall in behind.

When we arrive, Snow-Cave Man hobbles up to meet us. He and Father exchange words about the horses. Pointing to the bay, Father asks, "Has this horse recovered from the race? Is it in good condition?" Snow-Cave Man examines Little Bear's racer and nods his head.

A breeze lifts the gelding's mane as Father turns to me and says, "Get on."

I hesitate and glance at my brother. His hard-eyed stare triggers a little knot in my chest.

"Go on." Father's tone allows for no waiting.

I turn toward the gelding and stroke his dark neck, averting my eyes to show respect. The bay's ears flick back in awareness. Since I have never ridden the bay, I loop a single leather rein through the horse's lower jaw to have better control. I grab a hank of mane, crouch slightly at the knees and swing astride. I glance at Father for instructions.

"Show me everything he can do," he says.

I nudge the bay forward with my heels

and ask him in low tones to be my partner. He seems fairly responsive, prancing only a few side steps before settling into a walk. I aim with my eyes to show him where I want to go and use knee pressure and body leaning to reinforce signals with the rein. I lean forward to send him into a gentle lope around the meadow and bring him back to a stop in front of Father. At my backward lean, the bay steps back three paces.

I catch a glimpse of Snow-Cave Man smiling at me.

Father turns to Little Bear. "You should be learning from your sister." He says it with a smile, but no one laughs. Then he says, "I have decided to show her the racing-way. Your teaching will also continue. We will find out whether you or your sister is best."

A smile tugs at my mouth, but there is a knot in my chest.

Little Bear waits until Father turns to me, then stalks out of the meadow.

For the rest of the morning I become the focus of Father's attention. He teaches me how to use the single-thong rein for an extra measure of control, how to approach other racing horses in a turn and gain the lead on an inside curve. How to distract a competitor to gain a step, and how to pace a horse and hold back its strength for the final burst of speed at the end.

I am wrapped in my dream of father-daughter horse world.

Sleep after sleep, my learning continues into the summer of the Full Leaves Moon. Horse after horse is selected for practice. Sometimes I get a teaching, sometimes Little Bear. We watch each other's successes and failures. When displeased, Father rasps out a cutting remark. When pleased, the most he can muster is a grunt. With me, there are many grunts. With Little Bear, not so many. I take secret pleasure in these moments.

Young men from the village sometimes gather to watch. One morning a friend of Little Bear says, "She has a strange way of riding, with no rein." Another nods in agreement.

A brave named Charges Ahead answers. "Strange, yes, but see the control. I will wager horses on her if Ironhand puts her in a race."

"You'll need to own some first." They laugh. He joins them, his infectious chuckle producing smiles all around.

I am pleased by this but know not to show it.

Charges Ahead stands out among the band's young warriors because of his fearless acts—Snow-Cave Man says reckless—in dangerous situations. While still a boy he saved one of his father's colts by running straight at a crouched lion, sending the startled beast twisting and bounding away. During one buffalo hunt, while still a pup in warrior terms, he routed three horse-stealing Blackfeet raiders by charging them on his horse with a lance in each hand, howling like a wolf. His wealthy father, Two-Scalps, is second-chief for buffalo hunts.

Charges Ahead stands with arms folded across his chest, relaxed and confident. An unusually long eagle plume is thrust into a knot of hair on the side of his head. Athletic and well-muscled, with a straight-toothed smile and laughing eyes, he provokes glances from females, young and old. My sister, So-chee, is among them.

When the teaching is done, I bring Shy Bird

over to where Father is waiting with Little Bear and the young men. Charges Ahead flashes me a bold smile. I look away, heat creeping into my cheeks.

One of the young men points at Charges Ahead and says, "This crazy boy-warrior wants to bet on your daughter in a horse race."

Father grunts. "He may have a chance."

Charges Ahead grins. Little Bear stands still as stone.

I wonder what Father means. The following day, I find out.

At the close of our next afternoon workout, me riding Shy Bird and Little Bear on the bay, Father waves us over to talk.

He turns to me and says, "You will ride this black mare in the Falling-Leaves Moon Race."

I do my best to hide a smile, but fail.

Little Bear brushes a blade of grass from his shirt and without a word, walks out of the meadow.

Father watches him leave. "Now your brother will try even harder." He chuckles, turns to me and takes my chin in his rough hand. "He may succeed. Then you will have to try harder."

I try to think of how to respond, and finally say, "I will not disappoint you, Father."

A strange sound brings me out of my time-journey trance—a low moan from farther up on the red-cliff ridge close to where I saw, or dreamed, Lena's spirit-being. Knee aching, I struggle upslope to where she appeared. The old buck deer is there, gazing at me with soft eyes. But no Lena. The moan turns out to be nothing more than wind whining through a cleft in the rimrock.

I stop, sigh, and hug my arms to my chest.

I hope Lena's spirit-being has been able to hear my racing story. I want her to know how much she and I have walked the same horse-sprit path. She would feel my same love of Shy Bird, hands resting on horse shoulders, feeling their hot spirit, black mane blowing in the wind. The same race-winning joy. She would come to know the medicine of my path.

I must also help her know why I wanted her to follow her own horse-spirit path, not stray off course to join with the Alexander boy. It was for her own happiness. My path was cut short. Hers was still open.

That is why I arranged our get-away together, to bring her with me to the Bitterroot, to know my people and our horses. To keep her on her path. I was trying to help her, for her own happiness.

13

Snow-Cave Man

Snow-Cave Man swipes his antlers through a mountain mahogany bush and watches the ageing Takánsy wrestle with her memories. He hears the pleading tone in her thoughts. Does she hear it too? Does she know she is fooling herself? He stamps his front hooves on the ground to gain her attention. She ignores the sound and sits down, lost in thought-dreams.

His own thoughts carry him back to Takánsy's famous girlhood race and its aftermath.

As her father's teaching proceeds and their bond grows, she walks strong through the circle of lodges and greets people with eye-to-eye looks instead of eye-to-feet. She grows talkative, smiling at people she used to avoid. Instead of behind-the-hands jokes, girls seek her company.

Once Snow-Cave Man sees her come out of Aunt's lodge wearing a new white buckskin dress with prized cobalt-blue beads sewn into the sleeves. Wearing it brings looks from young men who used to ignore her. She is a fledgling leaving her nest, close to her becoming-a-woman time.

She spends less and less time with him. He continues to teach her horse-healing-ways, but the teaching grow less frequent. He resigns himself to her growing distance, but in his chest a crack opens. He misses her questions, her looking to him for advice, her confidences. He has come to feel protective of her, as would a father. Is it because he cannot seed any children of his own?

He has lived with the reality of his missing testicles for a long time, believes he has come to accept it, to be content with his lot as outlier. He is never going to have his own family. But the girl has taken the edge off his loneliness. And much as he hates to admit it, there is no mistaking the feeling her blind devotion to Ironhand stirs in him: *jealousy.*

Still, he feels happy that her dream-path is coming true. There is danger her chest will puff out with the thought that her good fortune is all her own doing. The sin of pride, as the Black-robes say.

And another danger, more worrisome:

Ironhand continues to set his children against each other. Snow-Cave Man wants to say this will not improve their horse racing skills. But he keeps his mouth closed and says nothing.

14

MOON-TIME

Three sleeps after Father chooses me to race Shy Bird, I awaken with spots of blood on my sleeping robe. My becoming-a-woman time has arrived. "Moon-time," in our talking-way. I leave Aunt's lodge to build a small moon-lodge hut away from our village, downstream so I won't pollute the water source.

Aunt explains all the rules to follow: Eat only berries and roots, no fresh fish or fresh-killed game. Do not touch meat from the head, kidneys or tenderloin of venison, or anything from beaver or bear. No touching hands to face to protect it from wrinkles. No touching my hair, to keep it from losing shine, or worse, falling out. No contact with others. It can weaken them, give them a sickness. Especially a man. If a man crosses my path, he can lose medicine, get sick, even die.

For four nights I stay inside, keeping the rule. But I feel restless. Bored with the waiting. Too hot in my blanket, I toss it on my buffalo robe. I step through the lodge opening into the cool night. The air hums with night sounds, crickets singing with no stopping, meaning no beasts or humans are prowling outside. I breathe in the rich smell of late summer grass and earth of the meadow bottom.

I want to visit Shy Bird. *What can it hurt? Everyone is asleep. No one will see me in the no-moon darkness. My bleeding is almost stopped. Surely it will not matter if I leave my lodge for a while. Tomorrow my moon-time separation will probably end anyway. I will then leave to set up my new maiden's lodge and prepare for my spirit-partner quest. Not just a trial quest, but the real one. Tonight will be my last chance to visit Shy Bird before the quest preparation begins.*

Mind-thoughts are very clever in finding ways to break rules.

I fox-walk down the path into the line of trees bordering the horse meadow. As I move silently forward, a figure suddenly emerges out of the gloom. A man is walking toward me about ten paces out from the trees.

I freeze, certain I will be discovered. But the dark form passes by without breaking stride. In the starlight I can make out a single feather pointing up from the man's topknot. Charges Ahead! The same young man whose smile sent warm waves into my face. Lost in his own mind-thought, he has not noticed my small rustlings in the trees, and the sudden quiet of the cricket people disturbed by my passage. I shrink back until he passes.

Shaken, I hurry back to my moon-time lodge. I think: You fool! *What if you have put the moon-curse on him? What if he gets sick and dies as a result of your impatience? What if he is killed because of your trying to visit horses before it is time?*

The rest of that night is a no-sleep night. My mind-thoughts haunt me with visions of Charges Ahead dying in different ways, each one worse. But to my great relief, no more moon-time blood flows that night.

At sun-awake, I remove my moon-time clothes and bundle them to be buried. I crawl out from my hut sore-eyed and drained. I vow to cleanse the mistake from my system with a sweat. Hope grows that my path-crossing with Charges Ahead has come too late to do him any harm.

15

QUEST

I take down my moon-time hut and return to the circle of lodges to set up my maiden's lodge and prepare for my many-sleeps spirit-partner quest. Ten sleeps alone, far from our village, fasting, praying, sweat-cleansing. Hoping for the all-important encounter with animals that will protect, teach and guide me through life. I hope for the horse-spirit. I also wonder if Snow-Cave Man's Jésu will visit.

Thanks to Father, I have help. He has arranged for Otter Woman to be my helper and virgin-keeper through the quest. She stays with me in my maiden's lodge for ten sleeps before I leave for Shining Mountain.

Having Otter Woman as my helper is a great honor. Neither So-Chee, nor any of Father's other daughters, have had Otter Woman for a spirit-quest helper. I am surprised to be worthy of such a gift. Father pays four horses to Otter Woman for her services. Four horses! I resolve to repay Father's generosity. I want more than anything to make him proud, help him win races, increase his success in the betting games.

Otter Woman's fame as a medicine healer is celebrated in people's songs. Her cures work their magic in many lodges. Only last winter, Chief Big Face's daughter survived a poison mushroom sickness after Otter Woman purged her.

Some children feel fright at first seeing the old woman's face. Thin and bony, with skin weathered and wrinkled as cottonwood bark. Two yellowing front teeth in an otherwise toothless upper gum, more like Beaver than Otter; sharp dark eyes that miss nothing. But her smile is warm and playful, the look of a mother river otter sliding down a mudslide, pups following close behind, playing with her, trusting her.

When I arrive back at Aunt's lodge, Otter Woman is waiting. With a gnarled hand wrapped around her walking stick, she waves me over to join her on a buffalo robe in front of a small fire.

"Come granddaughter, come sit. Have some pine needle tea. I brewed it up for your return. It will settle your stomach."

The tea warms me inside. I am eager to hear her words.

"So, Granddaughter, you have managed to get through your first moon-time without breaking the rules, yes?" She winks and gives me a two-toothed grin. "Or at least, most of them."

I feel heat creep up my neck. *Does the old woman know of my moon-time walk, my encounter with Charges Ahead?* If so, it does not seem to bother her.

She takes my hand. I feel I can put myself in her care. I vow to stay away from horses and devote myself to the tasks before me: setting up a new maiden's lodge, sewing my virgin cape, preparing for my time alone on Shining Mountain. With Otter Woman's help I will encounter the horse-spirit, claim it as my spirit-partner. Become a better racer and honor my Father. In time, I will find a husband whose bravery and wealth will raise Father's standing even further.

For the next ten sleeps Otter Woman teaches me. We build fires, share food, and speak about my upcoming quest—fasting, cleansing, being alone, staying open to animal and spirit visitors. When the talking time is over, I rise to leave, she chants a blessing and sends me on my way toward Shining Mountain carrying nothing but a change of clothes, bow drill fire makings, a knife, and hope for the future.

Oh, how my heart wishes for Otter Woman now, as I sit here on the red-cliff ridge waiting for another glimpse of Lena's spirit-being. After Lena's first-year death-day, I called on Otter Woman's spirit to help me remember the crossover ceremony. I tried to chant it at Lena's secret leaving place, just upslope from where I rest against this juniper, but I could not remember all the words.

Was Otter Woman trying to reach me when I brought Lena's stolen body up here? I remember wondering about the gray jay that perched on the stone slab when I covered her with rocks. There are many gray jays along the Bitterroot, but that was the first I ever saw here along the Big Thompson. I wonder now, does Otter Woman know where Lena's spirit travels?

A chirp in the branch above my head causes me to look up. My breath catches in my throat. A gray jay eyes me, cocking its head, black eye winking.

16

OTTER WOMAN

Otter Woman hops to a lower branch with a tail flick and flutter of gray. Winging through edge-world in bird shape is not her first choice. But no water, not even a trickle, can be found on this red-cliff ridge. No place for an Otter.

Below, Takánsy looks up with a glimmer of hope in her sad, gray eyes. Hope that cannot be satisfied, at least not yet. At some point soon, she senses, Takánsy will cross-over, and their spirits can talk with each other. Perhaps they can seek Lena's spirit-being together.

But first, Otter Woman knows there are too many holes in Takánsy's memory that need to be filled before she can find peace.

She remembers how eagerly Takánsy prepared for her spirit-partner ordeal. All open-eyes, anxious to please, quick to learn. But for the wrong reasons.

Otter Woman flies from the juniper branch out over the cliff edge and returns to the Great Beyond. She shape-shifts into her medicine-woman self and time-journeys to the time when Ironhand bargains with her for medicine help in Takánsy's becoming-a-woman passage.

Propped against his backrest in First Wife's lodge, Ironhand tells Otter Woman he wants the best for his daughter, but the flow of words that follow reveal his true aims: winning biggest bets, owning best horses, taking most wives. Marrying Takánsy to a big-medicine family for highest bride price to get more possessions. He is ravenous as a bear getting ready for winter-sleep. More possessions mean he can be more generous. More generosity means he might sometime become chief. Although he tries to hide it, his thirst to replace Big Face shows.

Otter Woman makes him pay plenty for her services. As the most admired medicine-woman in Big Face's band, she can command high prices. Some people treat her as a shaman, but she knows she has no special *sumesh* magic to summon the dead or invoke the power of spirits to control weather or harm enemies. That is the domain claimed by old Crazy Bones. She suspects his *sumesh* is based more on deception and slight-of-hand tricks than real medicine.

Hers is a practical medicine, based on years studying animals and plants with her grandmother. Now she is old as a grandmother herself, but without any grandchildren of her own. Her children all crossed over before they could marry. Now she is nearing the time of her own journey to the Great Beyond. A good life, she thinks, despite times of wailing and disappointment when her plant medicine could not save her family from the red-spot sickness.

She welcomes training the young ghost-eye woman, partly from curiosity. The girl's set-apart-ways, her races-with-horses calling, her closeness to the frozen-foot Black-robe believer, and her horse-healing skills—all of these things spark Otter Woman's interest. She is also intrigued by Takánsy's stubborn chase after her father's praise. The young woman is slow to learn independence, like an otter pup that takes the better part of two winters' teaching to fish and survive on its own. Mother-otter patience will be needed to guide this girl into stands-on-her-own womanhood.

Another thing. Otter Woman feels sympathy for Takánsy's mother loss. Her own mother crossed over when Otter Woman had only two winters. Happily, she had the good fortune of being taken in by her grandmother, who gave her both love and wisdom of the medicine-woman's-way. Takánsy has not had such a mother.

After the crossover of Takánsy's mother, Otter Woman was called in to help with the burial preparations. She remembers the troubling absence of a midwife who had left Takánsy's mother alone in the birthing lodge, remembers the sprawled body by the lodge fire, away from the birthing robe, cold hands outstretched as if fending off an animal. The surprisingly vast pool of childbirth blood under the mother's body. The desperate cries of the baby girl taken up in her aunt's arms.

Even as a child, Takánsy had those strange pale eyes. Ghost eyes. For many women, a topic of behind-the-hands whispers. To Otter Woman, a sign, perhaps, of big medicine. Perhaps this young woman can be trained as a medicine-woman, an herb-healer, maybe even step into Otter Woman's moccasins when the time comes. Otter Woman broods on these thoughts as she sends Takánsy on her way toward whatever spirit encounter awaits her on Shining Mountain.

Ten sleeps later Takánsy returns, tired and hungry. Otter Woman pulls her into her lodge and plies her with tea and a small amount of water cress and boiled camas roots.

"Come, Granddaughter," she says. "You have much to tell me, yes? But first, you must get some food in you. Not too much at first."

Takánsy picks at her food, then sets it aside. Otter Woman eyes her, senses confusion as well as exhaustion in the young woman's furrowed brow.

She leans close and clasps the young woman's hand. "You went to Shining Mountain, yes? By the rock waterfall, as I taught you?"

Hesitation, followed by a quiet "Yes." A pause, then: "I found a hidden meadow close by. Soft mountain grass. A small clearing, only a stone's throw across. A talking stream below the falls. Protected on two sides by rock walls, screened by trees where the stream enters and leaves. You can see anything coming before it gets there. Easy to escape if it is the wrong thing. A safe place. I felt good there."

Otter Woman nods. "Did you find any animal bones there?"

"I searched, but no. No bones."

"Any lightning trees? Places of lightning strikes have power."

"No."

"What about food? Did you follow the no-food path?"

Takánsy looks at the camas roots in front of her. "Yes, as you taught me. At first it was hard, then...now, I no longer have the hunger."

"Any visits by animals?"

"Three does. A skunk family at night." Takánsy's wan face blooms into a smile. "Big mama snaking through grass followed by two young ones, sniffing my lean-to lodge, finding nothing, busying along while the young ones played. Big mama trying to keep them in line, the little ones rolling and tumbling, ignoring her. Her finally leaving, the babies discovering she was gone, getting scared, running after her."

"No bear? Wolf? No coyote? No people? Nothing else?"

Takánsy shakes her head. "None of those. Some feathered ones is all."

"What about visions?"

Takánsy pauses, as if collecting her thoughts.

"Yes, but not at first. First sleep was full of hunger, second and third, waves of hunger pains, like knives in my belly, then third and fourth, weakness and mind-fog. Hard to continue.

"My stomach shrank into a hard knot. Then came body-calm, but still no visions. I was waiting...waiting...waiting. I almost gave up hope.

"Ten days!"

Otter Woman cups the young woman's chin in her hand. "You thought about making up a two-tongue story, yes?"

Takánsy nods, eyes shifting away.

Otter Woman coaxes her back with a soft, "Sometimes young people do that. They want a spirit-partner visit and when this does not happen, they have the fear-of-failure feeling and pretend. It does no good. You can speak two-tongue to others, but your own heart knows the truth."

"Grandmother, I prayed so hard for a vision! I fasted and bathed, did cleansing ceremonies over and over. I did not think my heart could get any more pure. I banished bad thoughts—jealousy, pride. And oh, how I sang my spirit song! Over and over. And finally, on the last sleep, when all but one of my ten counting stones were left..."

"Your vision came?"

"Yes. The horse-spirit."

"Just as you hoped. Tell me. Don't leave anything out."

"It was the last sleep. I was dozing. I got up and went to the trees to pass water. I had my medicine pouch with me, with the horse hair and crushed horse skull bone. I felt light-headed. When I looked back to where I had been lying, a horse was standing there."

"Mare or stallion?"

"A mare. A huge mare. Much bigger than any real horse."

Otter Woman bores her with her eyes, holding the young woman's gaze. "Color?"

"Red. But not like a normal sorrel horse. More...light. Edged with light."

"What did you do?"

"Just stood there. Probably with my mouth open. Not believing, but seeing."

"Then?"

"I started walking toward its shoulder. It turned and looked at me. Big kind eyes. I remember the eyes. I walked closer and it was gone. Just gone, like it was never there."

"Anything else?"

"Yes. Later, by the edge of the meadow, I found a big pile of horse dung. Steaming droppings big as war club stones. I touched them." Takánsy reached out her hand as if she needed to convince her medicine guide. "It was real."

Otter Woman searches the young woman's face. In her experience, visions do not leave such touchable evidence behind.

But she says only, "Go on."

"I am sure it was the Horse Sprit. I was so grateful. I did not think myself worthy. Then I sang my horse-spirit song. Sang and sang."

"What about the skunk people—why do you not think of skunk as your spirit-partner?"

Takánsy's nose wrinkles. "No, no. The horse-spirit is mine!"

A little too much certainty, Otter Woman thinks. But she lets the thought go.

"That is all?"

"Yes. Well, there was one other thing. My Shy Bird horse found me."

"*Hai!* Your race runner." Otter Woman finds this more real than giant horse droppings.

"How she found me I do not know. She pulled her picket stake. She was dragging it."

"When?"

"It was at the end, right after the vision. I was sleeping. There was a warm breath on my neck and a soft snort. Shy Bird. She woke me up."

"A long way for her to wander from the horse meadow, yes?"

Takánsy nods, looks down.

Otter Woman suspects the horse did not arrive at the rock waterfall place by itself. She reaches out to Takánsy and gives her a gentle shake.

"Granddaughter, listen to me. I know you sometimes feel alone. You are not like most young women. You sometimes feel closer to horses than people, yes? But you now have a spirit-partner. A powerful one. You can learn from the horse-spirit. Horses can teach you much about people, if you let them."

"Yes Grandmother, I have watched horses for many winters."

"Hush, hush. You have only just begun. It is a many-winters kind of teaching. You cannot just have a vision and say a few prayers and ask your spirit-partner for help and expect everything to go well. It does not work that way."

"What...how does it?"

"You have learned much about horses in your few winters. But you know little about people. You must now let the horses show you new ways. The horse tribe, they are herd animals. How do they manage to get along with each other? How do the different ones fit in? What does this teach you about people? These are the kinds of questions you must put your mind to answering."

"Then you must work to understand the people in your life. What draws them on their paths? What face do they put on for others to see?

What lies underneath that face? When they sing their victory songs, are they two-tongue stories? Do they act to help others, or serve only themselves?"

"Finally, and this is most important, you must understand yourself. Sometimes we believe two-tongue stories we tell about ourselves. We are blind to our own truth-twisting. We sometimes hide from it, like a colt hides behind its mother. Our heads believe we act for one reason, but in our hearts there may be buried a different reason, yes?"

Takánsy yawns.

Otter Woman reins herself in. The young woman is not ready for long talks from old medicine women, especially words that might lead away from the path she seems determined to follow.

"*Hai,* your body, she is wanting some sleep now, yes? We will do more talking after." She wraps Takánsy in her arms, wishes her a long sleep, pushes herself up from beside the glowing coals of the fire and waves Takánsy out to her maiden's lodge for a much-needed rest.

17

COLT-CHEWING

The gray jay flies away and disappears over the edge of red-cliff ridge. I lean back against the juniper feeling abandoned as a broken water jar. How I would love to speak again with Otter Woman! Almost as much as to find Lena. That crafty old medicine-woman taught me much. She tried to guide me along right roads. I did not always listen to her, set as I was on my own road. But her wisdom helped, especially in the horse race that Father chose me to ride in.

I time-journey back to my preparation for

that race. It takes place late in the full-leaves moon after my spirit-partner quest. Father continues to set my brother and me against each other as we train. I believe he is doing this for our own good, to make us both better racers. It helps me stay on the right path, working hard to be best. But inside my head is a nagging whisper: *What if I fail him? What if I lose favor?*

My other worry is Little Bear. Father goads him, a stick poking an angry anthill, and Little Bear's anger flares toward me. It gives me stomach-knots. I wonder how to dampen his fire.

I remember Otter Woman's advice to learn what my spirit-partner can teach me about people. An idea comes to me as I watch a young colt in a pasture with mares. The colt, a brown and white paint getting its running legs under it, stretches its neck toward a boss-herd mare and make a chewing motion with its mouth. At first the older horse bares her teeth and gives the ears-laid-back warning. But as the colt chews, the mare's ears relax forward and she resumes eating grass, allowing the colt to approach. I smile at this permission-asking behavior and draw a people-lesson from it.

During our next practice teaching, I try "colt chewing" in front of Little Bear. I tell him how well he rides. I ask him questions about his horse skills. When Father sets us against each other in practice races, I sometimes hold back a bit so my brother will win.

For a while Little Bear's anger cools. But Father is too shrewd to allow this.

"You are easing up," he shouts at me. To Little Bear he hurls word-spears. "You are letting a girl beat you!" Then, "See how she rides her horse!"

When the time draws near for the Falling-

Leaves Moon race, I use my colt-chewing-way to convince Father to enter me and my brother in separate contests so we will not have to race against each other.

We both win our races, me on Shy Bird, Little Bear on the bay. Afterward, Father gives me a smile. It warms my heart. I lift thanks to the horse-spirit and Otter Woman.

Yet the truce does not last. Father gathers in more bets on my win than on Little Bear's. And during the dance after the race, Father presents me with an eagle feather. Little Pony, the story-teller, sings a song about my race. Little Bear's eyes simmer like water before it boils. After a while I do not care anymore. Father is the stallion in our family herd. He knows what is best.

18

BLACK-ROBE

I time-journey back to the seasons between my thirteenth and fifteenth winters. The snows come, then the next Camas-Root Moon, then the late summer buffalo hunt, another snow, and finally, another Greening-leaves Moon.

Father's winnings are growing, along with his medicine. There is scattered talk of him becoming chief as Big Face ages.

My own standing in our band is growing. No longer Ghost Eyes, no longer Stays-With-Horses girl. Now Races-With-Horses Woman. I feel myself changing from a skittish yearling to a proud mare, head raised, tail high. I prance a little more than I should. I secretly enjoy watching people shift their gaze away from my gray eyes, rather than the other way around.

Yet my new perch does not quite feel safe. Father's approval is a weak branch. If I lose a race, it may break. At night I sometimes jerk awake with pounding heart and sweating hands, gripped by dreams of failure, of race-losing, of shame. Father losing his wagers. Little Bear smirking.

In morning prayers I bring back the horse-spirit. She lopes beside me during sun-time as I practice with Shy Bird. But defeat still stalks my dreams, a wolf in the shadows.

In the Greening-leaves Moon after my fifteenth winter, a runner pants into our village with startling news. A Black-robe is headed our way. Even now he is encamped in the valley west of the Mountains-That-Poke-the-Moon, which the Lightskin traders call "Pierre's Hole." According to the runner, all breathless and excited, he is none other than the chief Black-robe himself. He will meet us during the coming summer buffalo hunt on the Three Rivers Plains on the other side of the sun-awake mountains.

The message kindles much excitement in the followers of the Black-robe-way. They gather with Snow-Cave Man at the lodge of Big Face to launch their hymn songs and voice-prayers skyward, arms raised. Their numbers are growing. Half the people now believe powerful Black-robe medicine will bring hunting success, strength against our Blackfeet enemies, and protection against sickness.

Snow-Cave Man tells me the reason for their excitement. Although the Iroquois men who brought the Black-robe-way to the Bitterroot are able to teach songs and prayer words, they are not allowed to perform the holy water ceremony called "bab-tism." Only a Black-robe medicine man can do that. And only by bab-tism can people get Jésu as spirit-partner.

That is why, over the past eight winters, four small groups of Black-robe followers journeyed to a place called Saint Louis to bring a Black-robe to the Bitterroot. The first two groups failed. The third, two summers ago, ended with the murder of Old Ignácio and his companions at the hands of the Lakota people. The fourth try, Snow-Cave Man is heart-warmed to hear, has been successful. It is led by a man called Little Ignácio, who although he bears the same name, is not a son of Old Ignácio, just younger.

I wonder, do Lightskins have so few names they must share them?

I remember Little Ignácio, an Iroquois believer in the Black-robe-way. Many winters ago he and two others arrived in our Bitterroot valley to trap beaver for the Lightskins. Here he married a Salish woman and now has two young sons. They will be glad for his return.

Snow-Cave Man tells me he will go to meet the Black-robe despite his crippled feet. Even those who walk in the old ways, like Otter Woman, are curious to learn about Black-robe *sumesh.* For this reason, many who usually stay at our Bitterroot camp decide to make the Three Rivers trek.

Father, long past his buffalo-hunting time, commands First Wife to prepare her lodge for transport. Aunt will stay behind, but So-Chee and Little Bear will go. When the longest sun-day passes and the summer warm season arrives, nearly three of every four lodges leave our valley to begin the six-sleep journey through the dark canyon over the mountains toward sun-awake to the Three Rivers land of the buffalo.

I am among them. My first time on a summer buffalo hunt.

At our new camp on the Three-Rivers Plains, there is much talk about Lightskins. Many of us young people have never seen one. We ask old ones to tell stories about the first Lightskins to travel through our Bitterroot Valley long ago on their way to the great stinking waters toward sun-asleep. We ask others to tell us about Lightskins they have visited at far-away Lightskin encampments to trade furs for black powder weapons and stagger-water.

At last, our curiosity at a peak, Little Ignácio brings the Jésu father into our camp. The Black-robe is a short, round man with a round face. His hair, the color of sand, falls only to his shoulders. His eyes are brown, lighter than Salish people eyes but not as light as mine. True to his name, he wears a single black dress that covers his whole body in one piece, cinched tight around his neck and tied with a rope around his waist. When waving his arms he looks like raven.

Like ripples on a pond, we gather in rings around him, the inner one sitting, the second kneeling, the third standing, the fourth, where I watch, on tiptoe.

Next to me, Snow-Cave Man leans on his walking stick. Otter Woman kneels a few rows ahead. Father sits in the inner circle next to Big Face and Two Scalps, the father of Charges Ahead.

Little Bear and the other young warriors

cluster on the far side of the outer circle. Beyond them is the ring of lodges, and farther out, past the willow bushes that surround our camp, I see the vast yellow-dry emptiness of the Three Rivers land. It is hot there, and the air smells of dust. Enemy territory. I miss the green comfort of our Bitterroot valley with its mountain sentries.

The Black-robe stands in the center on a stump, Little Ignácio on one side, a wood pole on the other, with a shorter pole tied crossways about shoulder height. It matches a smaller wood cross that dangles on a leather thong around the Black-robe's neck.

Little Ignácio begins to speak. He gives thanks to Jésu for the Black-robe's safe arrival. His next words bring nods and smiles to the faces of his followers. The Black-robe, he tells us, will come all the way to our Bitterroot valley during the next summer moon. With him will come other brothers in the faith to set up a permanent camp and live among us.

Little Ignácio makes the touching sign and tells us that the Black-robe will now read from the Holy Book, then do a bab-tism by water for all those who seek to walk the path of Jésu. Little Ignácio will make go-between talk for the Black-robe, whom he calls by the name of Father De-Smet.

A murmur spreads through the Jésu followers as Father De-Smet pulls a black object from his robe and thumbs through thin white leaves with black marks on them. This is the mysterious Holy Book we have heard about but never seen. It is supposed to have powerful medicine. The Black-robe finds the markings he seeks and begins to speak. Then he pauses for Little Ignácio to repeat the words in Salish-talk.

My mind scrambles to understand all he says. There is a sad story of Jésu being hung up to die on a tree cross, mourned for three sleeps by his followers and his mother, Mary. Then Jésu comes alive again, and tells everyone they can also come alive in a place called Hea-ven if they confess their "sin" and follow his path. I wonder what sin is. I turn to ask Snow-Cave Man, but he is eye-fixed on the Black-robe.

Then I learn that sin means bad behavior and bad thoughts. Some of these are similar to what Salish people think are bad—speaking with false tongue. Failure to pray. Mating before marriage. But others stir unease. Having more than one wife is sin, he says. How, I wonder, can widows survive if they cannot marry into the lodge of their husband's brother's wives after their own husbands are killed?

He warns against gambling. My gaze darts to Father's face. He shows no outward sign, but I know his heart hardens at these words.

Crazy Bones, standing in the outer ring, cannot hide his dark fury when the Black-robe talks against hexes.

Instead of animal spirit-partners, Father De-Smet says we should seek protection from dead people he calls Saints. Why not both? I wonder.

Drinking Lightskin stagger-water is also a sin. This gladdens my heart, but not Father's. I feel him bristle without even looking at him.

Finally there is this: Jésu says it is wrong to hate our enemies and torture captives. Frowns and dark murmurs pass through the crowd. Some of the young warriors around Charges Ahead turn and walk out of the circle. Even some of the Jésu followers frown. Women who have lost husbands and sons to Blackfeet torture cast stubborn glances at each other.

As if sensing he may have taken a step too far, Father De-Smet closes his black book and announces that it is time for the bab-tism ceremony. He waves his wooden cross over a large pot on the ground in front of him and explains that the water in the pot, now blessed, has the power to wash away sin and take people to the beautiful Heaven after-world when they die, provided they follow the Jésu path while they live. Doing so will bring happiness, peace, and protection against sickness and danger. This assurance brings smiles back to people's faces.

As he describes it, the Heaven after-world sounds like a wonderful place, even better than the Road of Many Stars where Salish people go. Those who don't go to Heaven, he warns, will go to a different after-world called "hell." His description of the fire torture that burns forever without killing sends a shudder up my neck.

He then asks the people who wish to be bab-tized to form a line leading to the water. He asks them to promise to follow the Jésu path, then leads them in a prayer. Instead of looking up to the sky, he closes his eyes and bows his head down. Instead of arms raised, he folds hands together in front of his face. He makes the touching sign, then pulls another cross from his robe, a shiny silver one. A powerful charm, I imagine.

One by one the people who want to follow the Jésu path step forward and kneel before the water pot. The Black-robe dips out some water and pours it over their heads, saying words I cannot hear. Like our cleansing ceremony, I think.

I watch to see who gets in line. Snow-Cave

Man of course, along with all the Jésu followers. Quite a number of others as well. Not Otter Woman. Not Father. First Wife stands, but after a nervous look at Father, sits back down. My brother, Little Bear, walks over and squats beside Father. So-chee seems more interested in Charges Ahead than the Black-robe. She hovers near the young warriors as they amble off toward their horses.

I edge closer to the Black-robe, near enough to watch his face as he speaks his *sumesh* words and pours the sacred water. His smile is welcoming, his eyes warm and kind. I feel drawn to him.

I wonder whether his *sumesh* could add to the medicine of my horse-spirit. I know Snow-Cave Man would want me to walk in the Jésu-way. Maybe I will get the bab-tism during next summer moon when I am another winter older and the Black-robe comes to our Bitterroot valley to set up a permanent camp. Then I see Father, hands waving, Little Bear in tow, hobbling off toward his lodge, and I put that thought aside.

The Black-robe leaves us after seven sleeps. Many are sad to watch him go but take heart in his promise to return.

Our camp goes back to buffalo hunting. Little Bear swaggers over his two buffalo kills. First Wife's son, my half-brother, brings down another.

Then comes the women's work: butchering, skinning, meat-drying and packing for travel back to the Bitterroot. By the end I am exhausted, sweat-drenched, muscle sore, arms, feet and buckskins splotched with blood. But happy, feeling one with Father's family, with our band.

There are no attacks by Blackfeet raiders.

Many say Father De-Smet's *sumesh* is protecting us. Crazy Bones scoffs at this, crediting his own *sumesh*. Otter Woman thinks the unusually large size of our encampment has discouraged enemy attacks. Whatever the reason, we have a successful summer hunt. Our buffalo dance at the end is full of laughter, good-natured bragging and loud singing.

I dance in the women's circle, swept up in the rhythm of drums and chanting, my quick steps full of new energy. My hair is washed and braided, my skin glows with oil and smells of crushed purple prairie flowers. The men face us and circle in the other direction, smiling and nodding as I pass each one by.

When Charges Ahead circles into view, his eyes touch mine for a moment before passing on to linger on So-chee's swaying form. Flustered, I look away, heat rising in my neck.

19

CHARGES AHEAD

Back at our Bitterroot home, I think of ways I can weave more sinews to bind me to Father. I am now a woman, three winters past my moon-time. It is time, past time even, to wed. Father's chest will swell if I attract a young man from an important and wealthy family owning many horses and plenty goods for bride gifts.

To do that, I will need all the woman's-way skills I can master. Before, the teaching of beadwork and tanning and cooking felt like a heavy stone, a drag on my becoming a horsewoman. Now, I hope they might help.

But more is needed. I need to learn about the courtship-way. Aunt will be of no use. I need the guidance of Otter Woman. Her lodge is now set up next to my maiden's lodge. She has agreed to be my virgin-keeper, my guide and protector.

Father agrees to this, offers to pay for her services. She says no, she does not need his help. She now thinks of me as granddaughter.

I tell her I will help her in return. Clean her lodge, carry fire wood, help cook, help her gather and dry medicine herbs. We celebrate this agreement with a pipe-smoke ceremony. She laughs, pokes me in the side and tells me she knows a trick or two about catching a man, having had three husbands.

I know I am no beauty. That is So-chee's gift. Marriageable braves gather around her like young stallions, noses flaring, necks arching. Young men look at me with curiosity, admiration maybe, but not in the way they look at my sister.

One of these young men is Charges Ahead. The young brave I came close to contaminating during my first moon-time. His family is wealthy and generous; his father, a tall second-chief named Two-Scalps, has three wives and many horses.

The thought of him sends a flush up my neck. His muscles are hard, each standing apart from the next, rivered with veins. No fat on his bones. His walk is strong, sure-footed, a graceful young lion.

Other young braves buzz around him like bees. He has friendly eyes. Bold. Eyes that rove over young women during festivals and dances, alighting first on one, then another, raising blushes and look-aways.

When his gaze falls on me, as it did during the summer buffalo dance, my heart jumps in my chest.

Last winter Charges Ahead brought honor to his family during the buffalo hunt. He rode his father's buffalo runner into the churning danger of the lead animals. Brought down a big bull and two prime cows. By the end of his celebration song at the buffalo dance, every young woman in the band was ready to cut off an arm to get him. Including So-chee.

I banish the handsome young man's image from my mind. There is not much chance for a match with Charges Ahead. By the time I am ready, that young warrior's heart will be captured by someone more beautiful and more skilled in the woman's way than I.

My sister has her eye on him. She casts bold smiles his way. She walks by his lodge with her friends, singing, pretending no-interest, fooling no one. Everyone thinks that sometime soon, Charges Ahead will tie a gift horse outside First Wife's lodge announcing his wish to speak to Father about marrying my sister.

Father will welcome such a union. Not just for bride gifts, but for family ties. Two-Scalps is a buffalo hunt chief, something Father cannot do because of his bad leg. If Big Face falls to a sickness or crosses over, Father will need Two-Scalps's support for becoming chief.

One time Father comes to Aunt's lodge to talk with So-Chee and me. This is strange. I go hair-on-neck alert. It is a talk I will not forget. He moves to his place at the back of the lodge, sits down and waves at us to sit with him.

He asks So-Chee, "When will I get a visit from Charges Ahead?"

She shrugs, looks away.

"You are still a virgin, are you not? Two-Scalps will never accept a soiled mate for his son."

So-chee's hand flies to her mouth. "Father, I am still...I am not...soiled."

"Maybe your breasts are too big. Does your young brave prefer small ones like your sister's?"

Now I am the one with my hand on my mouth.

He winks and laughs. "Let us give Takánsy a chance at wooing Charges Ahead. Maybe that will speed things up."

So-chee does not laugh. She looks at me, eyes stricken, a wounded deer.

Father switches his gaze to me. "You are now a young woman of high rank, with winning medicine. Maybe Charges Ahead has eyes for such a woman. You should try getting him to touch you with his eyes." He shoots a sly glance at So-Chee, whose face turns white. "I am not pulling your braid," he says to me. "Do not fail, like your sister."

He shoos us out with a flick of his hand.

Outside the lodge I try to talk to So-chee, to say I am feeling bad for her, to explain that Father is only trying to get her to try harder.

She turns on me, eyes blazing, voice shaking. "It is your doing!" Her pretty face anger-twists. "You are casting spells on Father." She turns away, leaving me standing with my mouth open.

My heart grows hard against her. When Father seeks me out later and prods me to cast a courtship eye on Charges Ahead, I agree. Nothing would please me more than to attract that young warrior with the flashing smile. But I am worried. Although my spirit-partner gives me confidence, I know failure is likely. To get Charges Ahead to desire me, to touch me with his eyes, I need more than fame as a horse woman. I need big medicine—Otter Woman's *sumesh*.

To signal courtship interest, Charges Ahead will need to bring a gift, usually a horse, to Father's

First Wife's lodge. Marriage is not just between two people, but between lodges. Our two families must talk, consider good and bad reasons for a union, bargain over gifts.

Before this can happen, Charges Ahead must desire me. No one can force him. To help kindle the love feeling, young people or their families often ask help of a shaman or medicine-woman. People with *sumesh* for making love charms. But their medicine is not free.

That is the help I need. I do not think I can capture the heart of Charges Ahead without it. When Father sends me on the courtship-way, I am afraid to ask him whether he will pay for a love charm. All I can do is mumble, "I will try to touch the eyes of Charges Ahead. Maybe Otter Woman will have advice for me."

I set out to find Otter Woman, heart in throat.

20

OTTER WOMAN

From her juniper tree perch on the red-cliff ridge, Otter Woman time-journeys back to Takánsy's request for help with a love charm for Charges Ahead.

She is sitting in her lodge heating water over her cook fire. Three winters have passed since she became Takánsy's guide during the girl's first moon-time. She has grown fond of her young friend, whom she calls Granddaughter. They talk together of spirit guides, the Great Beyond, the power of medicine, and practical things like food, horses, racing, the doings of people in the band.

Takánsy has become her helper as well as her pupil. Otter Woman does not like to admit it, but she is becoming more dependent on her young ward for wood gathering, herb collecting, cooking, sewing and lodge moving when the band changes location, tasks increasingly hard as she ages. With no surviving children of her own, Otter Woman has a mother-daughter feeling she worries may be growing too strong.

She pulls a strip of willow inner bark from one of the bundles of dried herbs that hang from the wood poles of her lodge like moss on forest trees. Medicine for her aching joints, and something else she can't name: a shadow presence in her stomach, or below her stomach, that does not go away. Maybe willow tea will help. She drops the bark into boiling water and rocks back on her haunches while they steep. The pungent odor soon fills the small lodge.

She wishes Takánsy had more interest in plant medicine, but the girl's mind seems fixed on horses and horse racing. Not much interest in attracting a mate either. Otter Woman shakes her head. Her duties as Takánsy's virgin-keeper do not take much of her time, at least not yet. But that may be changing. Takánsy is spending more time braiding her hair just right, taking more care in dressing herself. More time bathing. Daubing pine-oil scent on her neck.

Her thoughts are interrupted by footsteps outside the lodge entry. The flap lifts, letting in a flurry of yellow leaves blown by a gust of chill air. Takánsy appears, her face in a frown.

Otter Woman waves her in with a smile, invites her to sit, asks if she would like to share the steaming tea. Takánsy kneels, rump settled on heels, and takes a sip. She exchanges a few words about weather and horses but moves quickly to the reason for her visit.

"Grandmother, there is something I need to ask of you."

Otter Woman smiles. "You have your eye on a young man?"

Takánsy's eyes widen, as if surprised at how Otter Woman seems to know her mind.

"You love him?"

Takánsy shrugs saying only, "Good wives love their husbands."

"So... You do not know him very well?"

Takánsy nods, a faint smile lifting the corners of her mouth.

"I want to know him better."

Otter woman sips her tea and appraises her young ward, who squirms like a fledgling out of the nest.

"Why do you want him?"

"Every young woman wants him."

"You are not every young woman."

"He's...handsome...and very brave...and kind, I think. He is a fine horseman."

"And a good stiff pole for mating?" Otter Woman grins at Takánsy's downward eye-shift. "Wealthy, too?"

"His family has many horses."

Otter Woman flashes another grin. "And they will make big bride gifts."

Takánsy shrugs.

Otter Woman laughs and reaches over to pat Takánsy's knee. "Your father will want big bride gifts to make up for what he has to pay me."

"Pay you?" Takánsy looks up, startled, and sets her tea down.

"You do not know your father asked me to help you with a love charm?"

"No, I did not...but why?"

"You are valuable to him, yes? You win for him the races. Now he wants you to win for him an important family bond." She pauses, grips Takánsy's knee harder to give weight to her next words. "But does your father care about you? Want you to learn the sprit path, want what is best for you?"

Takánsy looks away, pauses a little too long before answering.

"He has already given me much," she says.

"And you want to repay him?"

"Yes."

"This young man you want. It is Charges Ahead, yes?"

Takánsy flushes, nods.

"This will not be easy. Many young women seek his eye. Big medicine is needed." Otter Woman cups Takánsy's chin in her hand to spear her with her eyes. "It is said your sister has the eye for him. If you steal him away, her anger will be great. Are you prepared for that?"

Takánsy swallows hard but meets her gaze.

"My sister already has the anger for me. I am used to her insults. Slappings, behind-the-hands laughing with her friends. For her, my heart is stone."

Otter Woman nods. "Know this. If she goes to old Crazy Bones for revenge, you may need protection. He sometimes uses his *sumesh* to bring harm."

"He is harmless, they say."

"Most of the time yes. But there is still risk."

Otter woman pictures that old shaman,

a girl-man with falling-out hair and pocked skin even more wrinkled than her own, standing beside his strange, elk bone lodge just outside the camp's circle of lodges.

Takánsy bows her head for a moment, then raises her eyes to meet the medicine-woman's gaze. "The chance, I will take."

Otter Woman sighs and nods, sips the last of her tea. It has not calmed her stomach as she had hoped. She studies her young ward, notes her resolve, a young person's bluster.

"For you I will make the love charm."

The decision made, Otter Woman shifts to practical matters. "You must keep under blanket the place I go for the love charm and how I make it."

"Of course, Grandmother."

Otter Woman leans closer, lowers her voice.

"Tell everyone you are going to pick late ripening current berries for me. You will bring a picking basket. Our journey must be kept under the blanket."

"Where are we going?"

"To a cold place. You will find out soon enough. Do not dress too warmly, but hide an extra robe in your horse pack. And an extra shirt and breeches. You can ride my gray gelding. If anyone sees you, tell them I asked you to pick some berries for me. We will travel separately upriver. When you reach Otter Fork, turn upstream until you come to the first rock outcrop. I will wait there."

Otter Woman rises and waves Takánsy out into the crisp air.

"Go now, prepare. We leave after two sleeps."

After the young woman departs, Otter woman ducks under the hanging herbs and steps over to one side of the lodge to gather supplies: A digging stick. Several buckskin pouches. A small amulet bag. A weathered dress with her beaded medicine symbol—a red oval with six blue limbs. The Otter Spirit. Her source of medicine. The dull ache below her stomach tells her she is going to need that power.

The next day, Otter Woman walks upstream to where the Otter Fork enters the Bitterroot. She sits and rests against the white trunk of a quaking leaf tree and peers through a dapple of yellow leaves at the still pool below the river bend. Her special place, where she comes whenever she needs to renew her spirit. It is as familiar as the skin on the back of her hand, the place where she first encountered her otter spirit-partner as a girl just past her moon-time.

In this season of falling leaves, the river runs low. Upstream, where the water gurgles over stones before entering the pool, the river murmurs softly, a faint echo of its crash and rumble during the Greening Moon when the snow melts on Shining Mountain and fills the banks with turbulent flow. The air, crisp with chill, bears the scent of decaying leaves washed into eddies and drying moss exposed at river's edge. She fills her lungs and feels her body relax into waiting.

A faint *eeek* reaches her ears, answered by two smaller *eeeks*, sounds she has been expecting. They come from the opposite bank, an earthen cut, high as a horse, washed away by many spring runoffs. Atop the bank is a tangle of tree limbs and branches left there by spring floods. From under a dark opening framed by two branches, a short path leads to the bank's edge and down a steep slide to the river below.

She holds her breath as a furry face appears in the opening, black nose rimmed by light whiskers, two beady dark eyes below two tiny ears. The mother otter sits up, sniffs the air, looks from side to side, then sets off in her peculiar hunching gate toward the slide. There she pauses and turns to see her two pups tumble out from under the brush pile and run to catch up.

Down they go, sleek brown flashes that knife into the pool below and resurface as swift swimmers, heads above submerged bodies, thick tails snake-twisting behind. Otter Woman marvels at their ease in water, so different from their awkward gait on land.

The three swim toward her and haul themselves out on a gravel bar not ten paces from where she sits. Otters are not known for their keen eyes, but even if they spot her behind her leafy screen, they are so used to her presence she doubts they will pay her any mind.

The pups frolic, rolling and tumbling in mock battle to see who can get closest to mother in case she spots a crayfish in the shallows or a frog at water's edge. She nuzzles one, then the other, then bounds from stone to stone as if daring them to copy her antics.

Otter Woman loves how these creatures play. They never seem to tire of games, even when life becomes difficult, as it is about to, with winter approaching. Otters need a constant supply of food, their teaching has taught her. Their fur lacks the thickness that keeps beaver bodies from freezing, and unlike bears and badgers, they do not den up for winter sleep. They must eat every day. Yet they play as if the approaching winter is of no concern.

Otter Woman has done her best to follow the wisdom of her spirit-partner. She smiles at trouble, banters with those who seek her help, winks friends into laughter. She has fought off heart-fall each time she has lost a husband or child. She does her best to keep otter-play in her heart even as her own winter draws near. But the shadow-feeling in her stomach is not going away.

Mother otter stops her game-playing and glides back into the pool. With a supple thrust of her webbed feet she disappears under the surface. The pups watch her dive and return to their play. When mother reappears with a trout twisting in her jaws, they set off a joyful *eeeking* and await delivery of their meal.

They are slow learners in the lethal art of fish-catching. It takes two winters before otter pups are able to forage on their own. Mothers seem to indulge this behavior, but there is a limit. Next fall she will abandon them to their fate while she makes ready to couple once again with her wayward mate, who will leave her for other females in his wide territory as soon as she is heavy with a new litter.

In the meantime she devotes herself to teaching. Her offspring must learn to hunt for fish, crayfish, eels, grubs, mice, hapless ducklings in the spring—almost anything will do to slake their voracious appetite. Their lives depend on it.

When the otter family paddles away downstream, Otter Woman rises stiffly and sets off for the village. She has her own teaching to do, starting with the journey to Shining Mountain to fashion a love charm for Takánsy.

21

LOVE CHARM

I do not heed Otter Woman's warning about Crazy Bones. I brush it aside in my hurry to get the charm. I do have the love-feeling for Charges Ahead. My purpose is not only to please Father or punish So-chee. I very much want my young warrior for myself. I do not believe I can attract him without the charm medicine. That is what I tell myself as I return to my maiden's lodge to prepare to meet Otter Woman.

At sun-awake on the day of our departure, I dress myself and clop up the trail on Otter Woman's gray gelding to the rock outcrop beside Otter Fork. It sluices off the flank of Shining Mountain like a silver ribbon. Chill grips the morning air. Little clouds of mist puff from the gelding's nostrils.

Otter Woman arrives, lifts her hand in greeting, then turns her mount upstream. We climb all morning, and around noon, emerge above tree line, high on Shining Mountain. The sky is immense, a canopy of blue as intense as the beads on my dress.

At the edge of three tiny ponds sheltered in a swale on the slope of the mountain facing sun-awake, Otter Woman signals a stop. The ponds are lined with sedge and perfectly still. Sky-blue mirrors. I watch my spirit guide struggle to dismount. She can barely lift her leg over the horse's rump.

I jump down to help, but she waves me away. Her arms shake as she lowers herself to the ground. She hobbles her horse and signals me to do the same. Then, without a word, she peels off her clothes and steps into the icy water of the nearest pond. She turns, smiles and waves me forward.

"Our cleansing ceremony. Brace yourself and come in."

Hai! This is that last thing I want to do. But I strip off my shirt and breeches and step into the water. Shock waves slam my pelvis, then my breasts, then my shoulders as I lower my body into the pond. I copy Otter Woman's motions, raising my hands toward sun-asleep, then to the other three directions, twisting my feet into the pond bottom as I turn.

Brown bubbles tickle-rise along my body and burp to the surface. They release a dank smell, which overcomes the sweet scent of alpine fir and sedge grass crushed by our feet when we entered the pond.

The old woman's quavering voice rises into the stillness. She sings to Amotken, the supreme creator spirit, ultimate source of all medicine given to humans by their guardian spirits. She sings for acceptance, for a pure heart, for the granting of her request and for a blessing on the love charm she is about to prepare. She directs me to repeat the song, phrase by phrase. The numbness of my flesh battles with the rising of my hopes.

She takes my hand and leads me up the bank. The breeze raises cold bumps on my skin and sets my teeth a-chatter. Otter Woman's wrinkled hide seems unaffected by the chill. She walks over to our horses, takes out clean clothes from her saddle bags and puts them on. I hurry to do the same.

Still talking with the spirit world, she says, "Be pleased with these clean garments. They signify the cleanness of our hearts."

She takes the digging stick from her horse and walks along the uphill side of the ponds to a tiny rivulet that feeds them. The rivulet bubbles up from beneath a stone on the side of the slope where morning sun-warmth is strongest. At the spring, Otter Woman points her stick at some tiny yellow flowers of a kind I have never seen before.

She says, "Through these flowers the herb love spirit can be summoned. Tomorrow. At first light. Now we must sweat ourselves to welcome the spirit of the flowers, so it will not be offended and leave us."

She leads me back to the tree line where we gather dead wood and build a fire. When the fire is blazing, she directs me to put stones in it to heat. Freezing, I huddle near the blaze as close as I can.

Otter Woman points out how the stunted, wind-blown fir trees grow flat along the ground. They are pushed toward sun-awake by West-wind, their small trunks taking root again and again. "These are spirit-walking trees," she tells me. "See how Wind tries to kill them? But they know how to live."

She points to a bleached white stump at the windward end of a fir. "Before Wind could steal its spirit, this tree put down roots from its trunk away from the wind. When the trunk closest to the wind died, the new part of the trunk had roots to live. Wind still attacks the new rooted section, but tree always keeps a step ahead."

She points to a spot around twenty paces toward sun-asleep. "When I was a girl, this tree grew over there. It has walked to where we now stand and will keep walking until your children are old women. You should ask the spirit of this walking tree to help you be strong, help you keep walking when bad things happen."

I think of So-Chee and old Crazy Bones. I make a silent vow to be tough, like walking trees.

Otter Woman hands me her tomahawk to cut off a long piece of dead trunk on the windward side of the tree. I cut branches from six more walking trees, taking care not to cut too much. These she binds together at the top to make a squat cone-shaped lodge big enough to crawl into. Onto this frame we pile a thick covering of fir boughs, then spread our blankets over the top. Inside we lay more fir branches on the ground, leaving bare a triangle of scooped-out earth, a pit to hold hot rocks.

When the rocks glow red, we carry them with sticks into the sweat lodge and put them into the pit.

Otter Woman, looking satisfied with our creation, lowers a flap of blanket over the opening. Then she grins her yellow-toothed grin, strips off her clothes and walks once more into the icy water of the pond. I groan silently, but follow, shivering.

After another round of prayers, we make our way back to the sweat lodge and crawl in. Shelter has never felt so welcome. Otter Woman lowers the blanket over the opening. The heat of the rocks begins to penetrate our bodies as we sit on the soft fir boughs. Otter Woman sprinkles cedar and sage on the hot rocks, then some water. The drops sizzle and dance, like crazed bugs. Steam rises to our noses. Soon our bodies are pouring sweat.

In a quavering voice, Otter Woman chants to the Sweat Lodge Spirit. She sings thanks for the rocks' sacrifice as they weaken and crack. She sings thanks to fire for heating, water for cleansing, earth for the Sweat Lodge Spirit, and wood for lodge ribs. Thanks for the wisdom they give.

I began to learn the song and join in. The heavy, hot air is hard to breathe. I feel faint. Little points of light begin to flash, one after another, inside the dark sweat lodge. *The Spirits. I can feel them surrounding me. Will I be worthy? Will they help?* Hot mists swirl my thoughts away into the dark. For how long, I am not sure.

A sudden flush of cool air slaps my face. I turn and see Otter Woman lifting the flap on the sweat lodge entry. She motions to me to crawl out. We enter the pond, shock ourselves with icy water and crawl back in. We sing and pray for health and protection against sickness. Twice more we bathe and sweat. Toward the end, we pray for what I have come for—success with the love charm.

We leave the sweat lodge for the last time, wrap ourselves in blankets and lie down alongside a windblown tree. I fall into a sweat-drained, muscle-relaxed sleep, exhausted.

Toward morning I stir, turn and peek through a blanket fold to watch my guide's sleeping form. Her breath fogs the air in little rhythmic puffs. I marvel at the stamina of this woman. Her ageing body seems to gain strength from her Otter spirit-partner.

As if sensing my thoughts, she stirs, turns to me with a smile and peers at the lightening sky.

"It is time," she says.

We rise, break through the thin crust of ice on the pond for a quick bath, and put on our clean clothes. She leads me back to the spring with yellow flowers. We reach it just as Sun's first rays crest the ridge and reach across the sky to set the flowers ablaze with color. Otter Woman motions for me to sit so as not to block the light. An eager little tremor quivers through me as the old woman holds her hand over her heart and begins to sing:

> *"Plant spirit, you are of the earth;*
> *You carry* sumesh;
> *You soak up Sun and Water and Earth.*
> *All those powers are part of you.*
> *I beg forgiveness for disturbing you;*
> *With clean bodies and pure hearts*
> *we come to you,*
> *I beg you to grant us success*
> *in what we seek."*

With her digging stick she carefully pries two plants away from a cluster.

"You see," she says, "the flowers are like our village. There is a big one in the center, the chief. These around the outside are his band. This one with a yellow center is female, this show-off orange-centered one is male."

She shakes the dirt loose from the roots of one male and one female plant. From her parfleche bag she draws out a palm-sized obsidian stone flaked into a knife edge on one side.

"My *sumesh* stone," she says, holding it up for me to admire. "Sharper than any knife."

Struck by a ray of morning sun, the obsidian seems to glow with powerful medicine. It stirs a faint feeling of unease in my chest.

She scrapes a few shavings from each root and drops them into a square of white buckskin. Holding the two plants together at the base, she twists the roots together with the fingers of her other hand. Like lovers. A little wave of heat rises up my neck as I imagine myself and Charges Ahead wrapped together.

She tucks the entwined plants back into the ground and covers them with soil. Around their roots Otter Woman sprinkles some tobacco and places seven cobalt blue beads. Then she gives them a drink from her water skin and sings another quavery song:

> *Plant spirit, forgive us this borrowing.*
> *To take of your bodies we*
> *have purified ourselves.*
> *Please accept these beads as thanks.*
> *I implore you to join these two plants as one.*
> *Let them never part, even after death.*
> *Let the power of this bond pass to*
> *your daughter, Takánsy.*
> *Bring Charges Ahead to her,*
> *Let him be drawn to her like a bear*
> *to wild plum,*

Let him be bound to her as these
roots are bound."

As Otter Woman repeats this song, I feel
sumesh enter my body. I am no longer a skinny,
shy girl. I am a beautiful young woman, skilled
in the woman's-way, with my own medicine. I
imagine the eyes of Charges Ahead touching me.
I imagine his courtship flute whistling in the dark
as he paces close to my maiden's lodge, trying to
draw me out. I imagine his horse-gift tied outside
Father's First Wife's lodge.

A gentle nudge from Otter Woman brings me
out of my trance. She places the root shavings in
a white buckskin pouch, opens four bags from her
saddle pack and adds pinches of their contents to
the white pouch—some dark grainy powder, white
fluff that looks a little like goose down, fine gray
powder, a tiny pebble.

"This is the part I cannot share with you
unless you travel the medicine-woman road,"
she says over her shoulder. "Under basket things
handed down from my grandmother. Big *sumesh*,
yes?" She smiles her crafty smile.

I return the smile but hear the wish in her
voice. The yearning for me to become her apprentice
in medicine-woman skills. But we have had this
conversation before. I remain silent.

She turns, serious now, and shows me the
white pouch in her palm.

"Granddaughter, look at me. Listen well to
what I will tell you. This charm, it will not work
by itself."

A tight feeling rises in my chest. "Why is
that, Grandmother?"

"It is a powerful charm. But you have to
have your own medicine."

"I have the horse-spirit."

"It is more how you use it."

"What do you mean?"

"You must have noble purpose. Your heart must be pure."

"Grandmother, I bathe, sweat, do everything you ask. I pray to cleanse myself of jealous thoughts...of pride." Getting rid of pride is hard, I admit to myself. I do feel pride in my racing wins. I do love to re-live them in my thoughts.

"Your heart must want Charges Ahead for himself. To be a good wife to him. To help him along his path."

I nod. I do want these things.

"Your love must be pure, your heart right. Not doing it to please someone else. Not to make your father proud. Not to walk with high head and big chest in front of others. Not for revenge against your sister."

I think of Father's face: the smile he will wear when he hears about the courtship of Charges Ahead, when he sees the bride gift. I also think of the shock on So-chee's face, and cannot avoid a spear of satisfaction thrusting into my mind.

I feel my face flush as I look at the ground and say, "I understand."

"One more thing." The old woman's bony hand grips my elbow like a claw. "You must not be alone with Charges Ahead before the marriage ceremony. You must not devalue yourself and dishonor your family."

My cheeks flame. "Of course not," I assure her. Such an act would spoil everything, I know. I say, "There is no danger of that."

"Then here it is." Otter Woman opens my palm and places the amulet pouch in it. "Wear it around your neck. When you see a chance, try to sprinkle a little pinch of the charm into his food."

I caress the soft buckskin with my thumb.

"How much?"

"A few grains. It has bitter-taste. You do not want him to spit it out, yes?"

"In his food?" I try to imagine how to manage this, and cannot.

"If not his food, put some on his clothes, or his blanket, or even his horse blanket."

"What about inside his moccasin?"

"*Hai!* Yes, yes, that will do. Or in a fire close to him, where he is breathing the smoke." The old woman crinkles a smile and adds, "Make sure he is the only one close. You do not want the whole village to come courting, yes?"

I hold up the pouch, look at it in wonder, then tie it around my neck. It feels warm against the skin between my breasts. His moccasins, I think. I will put it in his moccasins.

Otter Woman's medicine is big. She sees into my heart. She is helping me, and I believe in her *sumesh*. Coming down the mountain before riding our separate ways into camp, I think about how to thank her. When I offer her a year of my labors as payment for the love charm, she reminds me that my father has already paid for her services.

Then, again seeing into my heart, she says, "I have a new doeskin that needs tanning. You help with that, yes?" She gives me her two-tooth smile and a wink. "We will work on it together while we are waiting to see if Charges Ahead comes courting."

22

OTTER WOMAN

Looking back on her matchmaking efforts from the Great Beyond and knowing the tragedy of what happened later, Otter Woman wishes she could comfort the old Takánsy, sitting against the Juniper tree in the edge-world. Help ease her journey into the afterlife. But she cannot. Not yet. She mind-journeys back to the time when Charges Ahead began his courtship of Takánsy.

Otter Woman is sitting outside Takánsy's lodge tending a smoking fire beneath speared fillets of salmon. Smoked salmon is not her favorite food, but the approaching winter hunger time doesn't allow choosiness. She hopes her nagging stomach pain will not grow worse from eating salmon.

Cottonwood leaves shimmer gold overhead. The morning air bites into her skin as she feeds more green sage wood onto the fire. Takánsy's soft humming from inside the lodge mingles with the sound of breeze-rustled leaves.

Ten sleeps have passed since Takánsy managed to sprinkle her love powder into Charges Ahead's moccasin. The young brave had left his clothing in some bushes next to the men's bathing area in a stream outside camp. Takánsy, flushed with success, told how she crept up behind the bush unobserved, dropped a pinch of love charm inside the footwear and returned to tell Otter Woman. Since then the would-be bride has had a hard time staying focused on the tedious task of rubbing deer brains into the hide they are working on.

Otter Woman smiles remembering Takánsy's eager mood. Belief in a charm's power is just as important as the charm itself, Otter Woman knows. This belief had changed Takánsy from a hesitant, timid yearling into a sleek, confident mare. Her developing female curves have helped too. They have not gone unnoticed by Charges Ahead and his young warrior friends.

The clop of horse hooves causes Otter Woman to look up from the salmon cooking pit. Through the wisps of sage-scented smoke she sees Charges Ahead stride past leading a well-muscled pinto stallion toward the lodge of Ironhand's First

Wife, where he secures it with a picket rope. A single eagle plume tied to a knot of his hair waves in time with his stride. A beaded blue stripe runs down the outside of his leggings, and a chest plate of ivory porcupine quills fronts his fringed buckskin shirt. Around his neck hangs a leather thong with a single huge bear claw strung on it. Clothing fit for courting.

She calls Takánsy from her maiden's lodge and motions her over to sit beside the cook fire. Takánsy's eyes fix on the young brave's receding back as she spears a piece of salmon onto the wrong end of a smoking stick.

Otter Woman chuckles and tells her to poke the fish with the sharp end. "Careful, granddaughter, you'll skewer yourself."

As soon as Charges Ahead ducks into First Wife's lodge, Takánsy grabs Otter Woman and buries her face in the old woman's robe to muffle a squeal.

In most families, the mother decides whether to accept a marriage proposal. But Otter Woman knows that contrary to custom, Ironhand makes all decisions, including the choice of mates for his children. Since Ironhand has paid for her match-making services, Otter Woman believes she will soon see Charges Ahead stepping out of First Wife's lodge with a smile on his handsome face.

But when the young brave finally pushes the lodge flap aside there is no smile. He does not look toward the two women by the fire as he strides over to untie his pinto and leads it away, his face a mask.

Takánsy's face falls. Otter Woman reaches for her young ward's hand.

"Be at peace," she says, although she feels

perplexed rather than calm. "These things take time. Some haggling is always needed."

She struggles to her feet. "Wait here." She hobbles over to First Wife's lodge, calls a greeting and ducks inside.

Ironhand sits alone, leaning against his willow backrest,the smoke from his pipe wreathing his glowering face.

"An insult," he growls. "The gods-be-damned whelp comes with a single horse, and an ordinary one at that. I will rename him Blunders Ahead."

Otter woman sizes up the situation and says, "No one is greater than Ironhand when it comes to the bargaining game."

He eyes her for a moment, then appears to accept this bit of flattery as his due.

"The foolish youth is desperate to fuck with my daughter, I will give you and your love charm that much." He grins at her through the smoke. "He will return with two horses, maybe three."

The greed gleaming in his eye repels her, but she masks her thoughts.

"You do not worry that the boy's father and mother will balk at the high price?"

"Ha! They are in thrall to their son's brave deeds and growing standing. They will give him whatever he asks for a bride price."

"But there is no limit?"

"I will not overplay my demands. There are other things at stake."

Supporting you for chief, she knows, but does not say.

"So the courtship will continue?" she asks.

"Of course. You can tell my daughter to keep doing whatever she is doing. It is working." With that he waves her out of the lodge.

Returning to the salmon smoking fire, Otter

Woman pulls Takánsy inside her lodge and creaks down into a squat. Taking her time, she pours some cold tea and motions for Takánsy to sit.

"What happened?" Takánsy asks, eyebrows in a frown.

Otter Woman keeps her eyes down. "Your father says no."

She hears Takánsy's sharp intake of breath.

Otter Woman glances up, grins and gives her young ward a wink. "He says no to the pinto. Yes to the courtship." She reaches over and pinches Takánsy's cheek. "All is well. Ironhand gives his permission for your betrothal to that young warrior."

"You are teasing me?"

"A little. So sorry, but it is always good to imagine bad as well as good outcomes. Your father rejected the gift. He is holding out for more. You must be patient. Charges Ahead will come calling. You will have a chance to talk, to explore, to know each other. All under my watching eye, of course. Meanwhile, the parents of Charges Ahead will meet with Ironhand and First Wife. I will make sure the gifting is agreeable to both families."

Takánsy nods, brows furrowed, absorbing this shift in plans.

"One other thing," Otter Woman says. "You are too eager. You need teaching in man-catching. Best to be uninterested. Plums out of reach keeps the bear clawing at the tree, yes?"

Sun-asleep. Sun-awake. Sun-above. Sun-times turtle-crawl into nighttimes. Otter Woman never strays far from Takánsy's side, like a mare guarding her colt.

Charges Ahead brings two horses to First Wife's lodge and begins his courtship of Takánsy. The first visit is awkward. Otter Woman sits between the two of them, helping ease their talk. Words are spoken about brothers, sisters, uncles, grandparents. She encourages Charges Ahead to talk of his hunting exploits, his courage on horse raids, his coup-counting on a Blackfeet warrior during the last buffalo hunt on the plains.

She prompts Takánsy to tell of her beadwork, her strength in hauling firewood and erecting lodges, her race-winning. She helps each say what they are proud of, without using the bragging-way.

More such visits, then a time comes when Otter Woman gives the two more space for private talking, within view but out of hearing.

23

COURTSHIP

I push away from the juniper tree on red-cliff ridge. My back is stiff from sitting here so long. My knees creak as I walk farther downslope, away from Lena's leaving place. I wonder whether Lena's spirit-being has heard my thought-speak, not sure whether I want her to hear all of it.

I time-journey back to my first courtship-alone moment with Charges Ahead.

It is close to sun-asleep. The shadow of Shining Mountain has already crawled across the valley and up the opposite hill, dimming light in my maiden's lodge. Charges Ahead sits cross-legged beside me, close, but not touching. Otter Woman peers at us from the far side of the lodge. Evening wind stirs the buffalo-hide skins beside the smoke hole into rhythmic flap-flapping, helping mask the low murmur of our voices from her ears.

Light from the small lodge fire flickers across Charges Ahead's arm and hand. I catch myself staring at his hands. Strong hands, lean, with corded veins binding hard muscles. I inhale his smoky male-scent.

"This waiting. It is a hard thing," he says.

"For me, too," I reply.

"Ironhand gives no answer." He frowns.

I poke the little fire with a stick and think of Father's shrewd face and calculating eye.

"He has many meetings with your family."

"Hmph. Many gifts to collect, I think."

"Your family has been very generous."

He spreads his fingers on one hand and raises his thumb on the other. "Six horses. And six beaver pelts. Not to mention beads and needles and small things."

"It is too much."

"Not too much for you." He leans closer, barely moving his lips. "Besides, it is not the gifts but the delay that wakens the badger in me. Back and forth, talk to this one and that one. Hmph!"

I suppress a smile. Otter Woman is right. I am fruit out of reach. His impatience quickens my pulse. Sitting close to him stirs a tingling in my stomach. Being courted this way is a thing to savor. I push the feeling aside, recalling the importance of this courtship to Father.

Before last sleep Father invited me to feel the rich fur of the beaver pelts and examine the other gifts. He asked my opinion about the gift horses.

He said, "This one may be a surprise in the races," and "That one will bring a good price in trade."

We are a team, father and daughter.

Beside me, Charges Ahead touches my arm.

"Why do you smile?" There is a trace of worry in his voice. "Listen, my heart...my thoughts.... You are there all the time. I cannot sleep."

I feel my pulse quicken. "You are in my heart as well."

"My beloved, come to me tonight. There is a place I know where we can be alone, down by the river."

My quick breathing betrays me. I feel a pull that is hard to resist. But I put a hand in front of his mouth and shake my head "no" while glancing toward Otter Woman, stitching a parfleche bag.

He pulls my hand gently down. A current runs up my arm to my throat.

"Please!" he says. "When she falls asleep. You know how to move more silently than an owl at night. Fly to me. She will not even...."

"No. No. It is impossible." I pull my hand away.

"But why? You have the love feeling for me, do you not? I cannot stand the distance from you. Please!"

I am unsettled. My pulse races. I force myself to remember my chosen path. I must not bring dishonor to my father. I must not ruin my hard-won success in making him proud of me. I must not squander his payment for Otter Woman's love spell, its miraculous success in winning the man who would link Father's lodge to one of the wealthiest and highest-standing families in the band. No rash impulse must be allowed to spook this quarry after so much careful stalking.

I say, "We must be patient. He will decide soon."

Charges Ahead slumps. He lowers his gaze and exhales a long, slow breath.

"I will speak to him after the Falling-leaves Moon race," I say. "When I win, it will be a good time to press for a decision."

"And if you lose?"

"I will not lose."

He frowns. "If Ironhand blocks us, we can make a runaway marriage."

Again I feel his pull. Runaway marriages are not unheard of. Two other young couples I know have done this. But they paid a price. The young man was not allowed to move into a lodge near his runaway bride's family. The young man's family would not speak to the bride. In one case, the couple had to move away to join another band. In the other, the couple never did well. Both brought dishonor on themselves and their families.

We sit a few moments more, without words. Then Charges Ahead rises, gives a stiff little nod to Otter Woman, and backs out through the lodge opening. After a few moments I stand and stretch, pace back and forth in front of the cook fire, then move toward the entry flap.

I cast a glance toward Otter Woman and say, "I will return after I relieve myself."

Her eyes, both sharp and questioning, lock with mine.

I give her a reassuring smile. "Do not worry, Grandmother. I am not up to any foolishness."

I step outside into air chilled by sun's descent toward sun-asleep. A neck prickle causes me to turn. So-chee is watching me from the entry of her lodge some fifty paces away. Beside her, cloaked in a black robe dangled with white bones that click when he raises his arm, stands Crazy Bones.

I turn and hurry down the path toward a stand of willows next to the horse pasture, a rabbit running for cover.

24

UPSIDE-DOWN FACE

I am too unnerved to return to my maiden's lodge knowing that So-chee and Crazy Bones are waiting there with their hex-stares. Even if I return, I cannot sleep. My heart is too unsettled by courtship close-talking with Charges Ahead. My suitor is impatient, as am I. Father's delay in accepting the joining-together proposal is wearing on both of us. I need to walk, to release body-stirrings.

I leave the stand of willows and walk down the familiar path to the horse meadow, where

I stop to groom Shy Bird and calm myself. She nickers softly when I leave her to continue along a trail that hugs the riverbank. My thoughts swirl like yellow leaves caught in river's current.

I have gone from riding in the shadows to prancing in public, from hovering on the edge of Father's world to basking in its center. My standing among the people is treetop-high. It is hard to avoid the bragging-way. I tell myself to take time to give proper thanks to my spirit-partner. Otter Woman insists on frequent prayer to remember that success comes not from within, but from the *sumesh* of my horse-spirit. I decide I will make a cleansing ritual at sun-awake, sing my *sumesh* song.

I worry about riding Shy Bird in the Falling-leaves Moon race. I will need all my spirit-partner's medicine. What if I lose? I do not want to think about what might happen. Would my new closeness with Father survive such a defeat?

I tell myself, yes. No one can be expected to win all the time, not even the best racers. Shy Bird is sleek, well exercised, and more fit than ever. Experience in a dozen races has calmed her skittishness and fueled her wanting to win. My own skills in the racing-way are sharpened through long practice with Father. I convince myself I am ready.

Three new buffalo runners will race against Shy Bird. Chief Big Face got them from the Nez Perce people who live beyond Shining Mountain in the land toward sun-asleep, people who are famous for fast horses. The three—a black, a bay and a pinto—are catching the eyes of gamblers in the village.

But I have studied the horses' habits, their strengths and weaknesses. Shy Bird will beat them, I tell Father, despite talk that at least one—the pinto—is faster.

Father plans to place big bets on me and Shy Bird, while goading others to bet against us.

"You are a bunch of women if you do not bet big on my Shy Bird," he tells them, with just the right amount of big talk to trick others into thinking he is worried inside. Or, "You are afraid that my daughter will beat Big Face's rider," he says. My alliance with Father grows ever stronger.

My wandering feet take me far upstream from the horse meadow. I walk away from the cottonwood trees along the river trail into another grassy meadow. The Road of Many Stars sparkles across the dark sky, each point of light an ancestor gone to the Great Beyond. I wonder which star is my mother.

A sudden movement on a grassy rise catches my eye. Two riders, briefly silhouetted against the star-filled sky, crest a low hill on my side of the river and ride toward me. Their dark forms—lumpy, oversized and strangely misshapen—seem scarcely human.

Fear spider-crawls up my legs. I stand exposed, no place to hide. Moving will only attract their attention. The ghostly riders disappear behind a small hillock, but before I can run, they reappear, closer.

Blackfeet warriors? Little Bear's nightmare tale, whispered to me when I was a child, claws into my mind: "They cut you. They take a dull piece of flint and saw on your cheek, or your breast, if you're a woman. They cut out pieces of your flesh-meat and feed it to dogs, while you watch. And if you're a man they cut off your cock and stick it in your mouth."

I told him he was lying, but Little Bear came

closer and leered into my face. "And if you're a girl they shove burning sticks up where you piss."

At this outrage I ran away. Later I asked Aunt about it, hoping for a denial. She said it was true.

The riders, a mere hundred paces away, turn from the meadow toward the river trail. The grass frogs fall silent at their approach, then resume their night chants after their passing.

I start breathing again. The horsemen did not see me! I glance down at my buckskin clothes. In the almost-dark it appears the same color as the drying meadow grass. I fox-walk toward the welcoming cottonwoods while keeping my eyes fixed on the retreating horsemen. I reach a shaggy-barked tree and wrap my arms around it. I launch a thank-you prayer to my Horse Sprit through the canopy of rustling leaves.

My mind-fear gives way to questions. *Why would two lone Blackfeet warriors ride the river trail this time of year?* Our village bristles with warriors returned from the summer buffalo hunt. Blackfeet raiders usually come when old ones and young ones are left behind in the village. If they catch people alone or in small groups, they kill the old ones and take away women and children for slaves. But that almost never happens during Falling-leaves Moon.

Besides, there is something not quite warrior-like about the riders. True, I never have seen a Blackfeet warrior in the open. I saw a dead Blackfeet once and examined a Blackfeet scalp. I know two Blackfeet slave girls in the Pend d'Oreille camp. But those lumpy forms do not look like wolf scouts for a war party.

The sound of a horse hoof pawing in the rocky river shallows increases my doubt. No war party allows such a noisy announcement of its arrival. Curiosity chases away my fear. Within the protective cover of the cottonwoods, I move from trunk to trunk toward the sound. A half moon begins to show above the sun-awake mountains.

Through a filter of leaves I make out two animals silhouetted against a starlit riffle on the water. Instead of two riders I see only one. The second turns out to be a towering pack tied to the back of a mule. The mule paws at the water, as if protesting his heavy load.

I creep closer. In the growing light of the rising moon, the features of the real rider make my eyes go big. An oval face with light skin. A huge growth of hair on his cheeks, lips and chin. Wolfskin clothes, beaver hair headdress, buffalo hide pack, and a deer hair parfleche with a black powder weapon poking out from under it. Fur-rimmed moccasins set in stirrups.

A forest-full of animals had died to clothe this man. The garb makes him as lumpy as the pack. A Lightskin trader. A no-danger trader. I never have seen such a man, but believe they are not dangerous because Father once visited them. My grip on the tree trunk slowly relaxes.

The Lightskin pulls back on the rein—no, on two reins—and says something that sounds like "*whoa.*" He swings his right leg high over the black-powder weapon and the horse's rump and lowers himself to a flat rock in the shallows. He squats down on the rock and takes off his hat.

My eyes fly open wide. He is scalped! No hair on his head! Are Blackfeet raiders lurking downstream after all? But there is no blood on his head, just pale skin. Maybe not scalped. Maybe this is how Lightskins look. Maybe their hair somehow moves from the tops of their heads to the bottoms of their faces. Maybe their heads are on upside down!

The man splashes his upside-down face with water, then the top of his head, water running down his naked crown like rain off Shining Mountain. His eyes sweep the line of trees where I am hiding and pass me without stopping. Upside-down-Face rises, shakes water off his hands, mounts, turns his horse onto the riverbank trail and rides toward our village.

I run ahead through the trees along the river edge into the horse meadow. The first person I see is Snow-Cave Man.

Panting, I stop and whisper, "Lightskin, coming with big trader pack. Upside-Down-Face!" Before he can respond, I run past him to Otter Woman's lodge beside mine.

"Grandmother! Trader! Upside-Down-Face!"

Two girls, up long past their sleep time, edge closer to listen.

Otter Woman steps through the entry flap and hobbles over to grasp my arms.

"You look like a horse in a thunderstorm, tail up and eyes wild. What is it?"

"A Lightskin trader. I thought he was two Blackfeet warriors, but it was just one with two horses; I mean a horse and a mule and a big pack, and he stopped and took off his headdress and he drank and I was so scared and...."

"What do you mean, 'Upside-Down-Face?"

"No hair. His scalp is gone." I pat the top of my head. "I mean his hair is all down here." I pat my cheeks and chin. "Upside-Down-Face."

A yellow-toothed grin spreads across Otter Woman's face. It triggers my own smile.

"Upside-Down-Face," the old one repeats, grin widening. The two girls giggle.

The laughing spirit suddenly seizes me. I try to hold it back but feel giddy, out of control. Laughter spills out like water from a broken dam, doubling me over, seizing my throat. Knees shaking, I sink to the ground, tears leaking from my eyes. I sit crumpled until the spasm of laughter passes, then peer wetly up at Otter Woman, whose grinning gums set me off again.

"Upside-Down-Face," I gasp.

The two girls scamper off, laughing, to spread the news. "Upside-Down-Face," they echo.

"Papín," says Otter Woman.

"What?"

"Papín. The Lightskin. He calls himself 'Papín.'"

"Papín." I try saying the strange word.

"I saw him once before, at the Pend d'Oreille camp." Otter Woman extends a frail hand. "Come, Granddaughter. It is time for sleep. In the morning the Lightskin will smoke with Big Face and come into the circle to talk and show his trade goods. We will want to see what marvels he brings." She waves me to my feet. "You have had enough excitement for this night."

Feeling pleasantly drained, I push myself up from the ground and step over to my maiden's lodge. I lie down on my robe and close my eyes. The evening gave me two tests, temptation, then fear, and I have overcome both. My sleep is as untroubled as a baby's.

25

PAPÍN

I arise to the smell of camp smoke partly washed away by a morning shower. The air is crisp and cool. I go with Otter Woman to sit in the inner circle of elders gathered in front of Big Face's lodge. No place for a young woman, but I am a virgin under the medicine-woman's protection, allowed to sit with her. Off to my left, Snow-Cave Man leans on his walking stick.

On the other side of the circle, Charges Ahead jokes with his young friends. I catch his eye; we exchange a quick smile, then I look away, properly modest. From the outer circle, people crane their necks toward the center. Graying elders, trophy-bedecked warriors, women in plain dress and braided hair, self-conscious young people eyeing each other, mothers with babies in cradleboards.

What draws their curiosity is a lumpy mound of trade goods covered by blankets. Birds, dogs and people call to each other, excited sounds of waiting. Squealing children run here and there. One child, a troublemaker, runs to the mound, lifts a blanket corner for a forbidden peak, and scampers off before anyone can stop him.

Our chief steps out of his big lodge, followed by the Lightskin, Papín.

"They say the Lightskin comes from warm-ward," Otter Woman says to me in a low voice. "He brings news of Blackfeet raids against the Snake people."

"So far from Blackfeet lands?"

"They carry many black-powder weapons. It makes them brave. Lightskins farther toward Sun-awake have much trade with the Blackfeet."

I shudder, remembering my fright when first seeing Papín.

"Our chief is urging more guards for the horse meadow." Otter Woman points across the circle to the young warriors standing beside Charges Ahead. "Those braves are taking turns watching horses at night. Let us hope none fall asleep after this long trading."

I decide to picket Shy Bird beside my maiden's lodge at night.

I glance at Snow-Cave Man, thinking he will have company in the horse meadow. I worry about his lame feet. He would have no chance in a Blackfeet raid.

Following my glance, Otter Woman says, "Snow-Cave Man will move his lodge back into the circle. Safer there."

I nod, feeling better.

Big Face brings Papín into the circle to stand next to the stack of trade goods. The chief lights his pipe, points it in the four directions and takes four puffs before passing it to the Lightskin, who puffs in turn then sends it on around the circle of elders. As the smoke rises, silence falls.

Big Face gets up, beckons to Little Ignácio, his go-between talker, and begins welcome words. He pauses after a moment so that Little Ignácio, with wrinkled brow and closed eyes, can repeat the talk with signs and strange-sounding Lightskin words for the trader to understand the message of our Chief. Little Ignácio is animated and forceful. I wonder if he is doing a better job at giving the Chief's talk than the Chief himself.

"I wish him to hurry!" I mutter to Otter Woman behind my hand. "Our Chief's talking-way goes on and on."

"The go-between talk gives him too much time to think of something else to say," Otter Woman whispers, giving my arm a squeeze.

As Big Face and Little Ignácio take turns speaking, I study the Lightskin. He appears to be younger than Father. Except for the beaver fur hat, he has shed his hairy coverings and replaced them with leggings decorated with unusual silver circles the size of aspen leaves, and a bright red calico shirt. Three knives are tucked into his belt, each with a handle and scabbard decorated with red stones that gleam. Necklaced beads cascade down his chest; bands of a shiny metal jangle on his arms. Big medicine. They make us hunger for seeing what lies hidden in the pile of trade goods.

In this garb Papín appears trim and muscular. Despite the strange face hair, his features and bearing attract women's stares. His eyes are brown. Some of the first Lightskins who visited the valley had blue eyes, people say.

This Papín man seems able to focus respectfully on the Chief's long talk while at the same time taking in all around him with commanding eyes. At one point he looks directly at me, his gaze lingering long enough to leave me feeling like a rabbit caught in a coyote's stare.

At last Big Face sits down, and the Lightskin begins to talk. His sign-talk adds strength to his words, which Little Ignácio repeats in Salish-tongue. His name is Papín, he says, and he thanks Big Face and the Salish people for their hospitality, bravery, honesty, and wisdom. No other tribes can match the Flathead people for these qualities.

"Flathead?" I whisper.

"It's what the Lightskins call our band of Salish people," says Otter Woman behind her hand.

Papín makes more nice-talk about us, then starts telling his own adventures and narrow getaways in bringing his truly marvelous trade goods to share with the deserving Flathead people.

He then stretches his arms toward the blanket-covered mound, walks forward and grabs one end of the cover. He holds it, suspended, while Little Ignácio tells us what he has spoken:

"My trusted friends, my brave and honest Flathead people, I will now reveal the wonders I have come to show you."

He sweeps the blanket aside in a great arc worthy of the best storytellers. "Aaahhhhhh!" breaths the crowd. Otter Woman clicks her tongue. I strain forward with everyone else.

Before us looms a stack of trade goods which he proceeds to lay out on the grass: wool blankets with red and white trim, black pots and kettles, splashes of colorful calico fabric, shirts, some red, some blue, fashioned from the same fabric, two small shiny rings of metal surrounding something clear, like ice, numerous small boxes containing... who knows? Beads in profusion, probably...maybe needles and fishhooks, too, then knives, mostly plain but some like the ones in his belt, adzes, tomahawks, metal scrapers, a spyglass, two long-barreled black powder weapons poking up from the heap like horns, and a brown wood cask with a stopper in one end. At the sight of the weapons, several warriors rise and point. At the sight of the cask, Father rises and points.

"Stagger-water," Otter Woman whispers.

Papín takes two steps forward, sweeps the beaver-fur headdress off his head and bows from the waist, first toward the chief, then toward the other four directions, his no-hair head gleaming in the sunlight.

At this startling sight, hands fly up to conceal smiles, and the words "Upside-down-face"—*Skee-wat-nos*—begin to pass from person to person like wind singing through pines, until they reach the ears of the trader. The wave of laughter threatens to trigger my own, but I am stopped by the realization that I am the source of the name.

Papín turns to Little Ignácio. "*Skee-wat-nos?*" he pronounces, then asks in sign, "What does it mean?"

Little Ignácio looks desperately at Big Face and signs, "It means...it means...'Soaring-Eagle.' It is a name the people call you...a name of honor."

At this bit of creativity, people look at each other or down at the ground or up to the trees, struggling to present a polite face, many of them failing. Heads turn aside into shoulders, and shoulders shake.

"And to whom do I owe this honor?" Papín signs, a smile tugging at his thin lips.

All eyes turn on me, followed by Little Ignácio's pointed finger.

"This is Takánsy , daughter of Ironhand," he signs.

I feel a push from Otter Woman. "Stand," she hisses.

I stand, head bowed, throat tight, heat flooding my neck and face. I peek up and see Father looking stern, Little Bear looking grim, Aunt fluttering, Charges Ahead winking and Snow-Cave Man smiling his lop-sided grin.

Then cautiously, I look at Upside-down-face, expecting to see bewilderment, maybe anger, hopefully humor. Instead I see a penetrating look of deep interest, a man's look, touching me with his eyes.

26

THE HEX

Seven sleeps after Papín's arrival comes the time for the Falling-Leaves Moon race. Dark clouds bully their way across Shining Mountain, spreading vulture wings over the racing meadow. The air quivers with thunder sparks. Astraddle Shy Bird, muscles tight, I wait for the race to begin. My stomach is in my chest.

Next to me, behind the starting rope, the big Nez Perce pinto paws the ground. Further down the line a dozen other horses dance into the starting position, riders tense. On either end of the start rope people gather to watch. Papín is there, hand-talking, head-bobbing, smiling at our chief, waving to women on the other side. Waving at me.

Beyond them in the betting enclosure, Father limps back and forth, cajoling, challenging, enticing. The bets are piling up. Much is at stake in this race, more than any other. During the time leading up to the race, Father has been bringing in more horses and more bettors than ever gathered in the racing meadow. He is counting on me to win it. I am counting on a win to get his blessing for my union with Charges Ahead.

Since the early spring races, Father has used his mind-bending *sumesh* to convince bettors that I might not win. In two previous races with low betting stakes, he told me to lose on purpose. With hidden movements of my legs and hands, I guided Shy Bird to end up second place in one race and third in another. Shy Bird did not like this, but she does what I ask.

No one noticed my tricks. Father was pleased. My heart was warm with this under-blanket planning. Visions of winning, of Father's bragging about me as he collects his bets, of his growing wealth and stature, of his acceptance of Charges Ahead's proposal, float into my dream-catching moments during rests between teaching times.

Now the time is here for dream-catching to become real. The drummers approach the starting rope. That is when I feel the first tremor, barely noticeable, running through Shy Bird's withers and down into her front legs. I lean down and press my palm against her quivering shoulder. Is she tail-in-the-air excited, as horses are before a thunderstorm? Or is something wrong? A sickness coming on fast? Not long before, as I walked Shy Bird around the circle of lodges, she seemed fine.

Another tremor, bigger this time. It travels from Shy Bird's body through my hand and up my arm into my throat.

What if Shy Bird is sick? Should I tell Father? Get out of the race and pull back the bets? My mind teeters between fear of disappointing Father if I withdraw, and fear of losing the race if I stay in. There is no time to puzzle the choice. No time for talking with Snow-Cave Man or Otter Woman. No time to pray to my horse-spirit for guidance.

The drum crashes, the rope drops, Shy Bird leaps forward. Drumming hooves muffle a distant roll of thunder as a fat rain drop hits my cheek. The race is on.

As we approach the first turn, I feel Shy Bird laboring to maintain the lead. Gobbets of grass-green saliva fly out of her mouth, flecking her neck and sides. A dollop of foam hits my forehead. I wipe it away, but its smell clings like sour breath.

One by one, horses pass me by. Shy Bird staggers, about to fall! I rein in, jump off her dripping back, grab her rein and pull her forward. I scream "No, no lie down" even as she goes down on one trembling knee. I jump to her side and drive my foot into her ribs. I fear colic, killer of horses who can't remain on their feet.

I yank sideways on the rein while kicking her sides and flanks. She looks at me with frothed mouth and glazed, bewildered eyes. I scream for her to stay up and move, pushing with all my strength to keep her from toppling over. With a vast shudder, she catches herself, pushes up from her knee and takes a shaky step forward.

"Keep walking, keep walking," I plead, pulling her along as I back up. Gradually her legs stop quivering and her eyes clear. I breath a prayer of thanks.

I pull Shy Bird away from the racing meadow. My eyes search for Snow-Cave Man and Otter Woman, but all I see are people milling about the finish line as the racers cross, shouting and waving arms in the rain that now gushes down like a waterfall. Thunder sends everyone running for cover. One of those violent storms that quickly pass.

By the time I reach my maiden's lodge the black cloud has glided away toward sun-awake and shed its last few drops. A rainbow appears, mocking the storm's gloom.

I grab a blanket from inside my lodge and began rubbing the water and foam off Shy Bird's back. She droops spraddle-legged at first, but gradually straightens. The light returns to her eyes. Whatever it was that nearly brought her down seems now to be leaving as suddenly as it came.

She nickers softly, reaches down and begins to mouth a tuft of grass. It is as if the storm spirit seized her and let go as it passed. Something unnatural. I feel the hair on my neck stand up. Shy bird looks at me and shakes her head. I give her one more rub and picket her next to my lodge.

I duck inside and pace in circles around the dead fire pit. Father's losses will be staggering. Will he accept my explanation that a sickness spirit suddenly weakened Shy Bird? I hardly believe it myself. I am supposed to be a horse healer who should know if her horse is sick. *Why did I not know? Why did I choose to race? Did my spirit-partner desert me? Or was I so blinded by thoughts of winning, so caught up in dream-catching visions of victory, that I failed to hear horse-spirit's warnings?*

I must talk to Otter Woman. I cannot wait for her to return to her lodge. Darkness will soon descend. The shadow of Shining Mountain has already crept half-way up the side of the lodge. I step outside to check Shy Bird. She seems fine, breathing evenly. I stroke her neck and back and leave her to go find Otter Woman.

Before I walk ten paces, I see the last person I want to see: So-chee. She hurries up, eyes gleaming, lips twisted into a non-smile.

"Father says to come at once to his lodge," she says. "No delay if you hope to not feel his anger." Her bird-eyes scour my face, looking for wounds. Despite myself, I feel my lips quiver. She spins around and walks away with victory steps.

I follow her into the gathering twilight. My feet are stone. My mind gropes for a talking-way to explain Shy Bird's sudden sickness, her greenish frothing mouth, a sickness spirit new to me. Will he believe me?

At the entrance to Father's lodge I stop. "Enter," he commands. I step inside. The light from the lodge fire, popping sparks, flickers on the hard bones in his face. His eyes blaze orange. "Come here," he says.

I cringe forward, staring down at his moccasins. "Father, I..."

His blow strikes with no warning. The side of my head bursts in a flash of light. The next moment my tongue tastes dirt on the lodge floor. Blackness circles the edge of my vision and begins to widen. I glimpse the flutter of Aunt's hands reaching out to me from the dark wall of the lodge. I see Little Bear and So-chee, eyes glowing, crooked smiles on their faces. Then the black circle closes.

27

IRONHAND

Ironhand snakes out his tongue over parched lips. A futile gesture, as there is no wetness in his mouth. His tongue feels thick and dry as the warty skin of that toad squatting a few paces away under a cholla cactus. Both he and the toad seek refuge from the searing heat in the shadow of a lodge-sized boulder, the only shade in this god-bedamned desert afterworld.

He seizes his war club, reaches over and smashes the toad into the sand, sending a squirt of foul-smelling guts onto his bare leg. He stands to wipe it off and accidentally brushes against the cactus, which, as if on purpose, leaves one of its spiny arms embedded in his shoulder. Dog Fuck!

How can he live in this place with no water? What evil force keeps him eternally thirsty without killing him? A foolish question, as he is already dead. His constant thirst is driving him mad. And it's not just for water. Lightskin stagger-water is what he lusts for. It fills his thoughts, waking and sleeping, with visions of cups and casks and Lightskin glass bottles filled with the amber liquid spilling onto the ground, just out of his reach. There will be plenty of it in the Great Beyond, if only he can get there.

He mind-journeys back to the Lightskin rendezvous on the Sis-kee-dee river where he first got a taste of the drink. The giddy release, the violation of forbidden acts, the wild mating with camp-follower women, the escape from worries old and new, the collapse into dreamless sleep.

The next-morning stomach heaves and head-hurting. Not pleasant, but never bad enough to stop him from the next bout of drinking. The problem was the long wait between drinks. The Lightskin rendezvous happened only during the summer moon and required long travel. By the time of Papín's visit, it was easier to get the drink from traders passing through the Bitterroot valley. But costly. The drink was making it harder and harder to build up his wealth and keep up the generous gift-giving necessary to become chief.

Oh, how he would have loved becoming chief! That would have finally wiped away the memory of the withering scorn in his father's eyes that haunted his boyhood.

The taunts still stung, even more than the beatings: "You are a coward." "You cringe like a dog in front of your brother." "You will never be a warrior worthy of my name." "You have the voice of an old woman." On and on. Even after he proved his father wrong by slaying three Blackfeet raiders, his father blamed him for getting his leg wound. "Your warrior times are over," he had sneered.

Then his father died, but his ghost continued the bad-talk inside Ironhand's head. Becoming chief would have silenced the cursed demon.

Ironhand knows he would have become chief if his foolish daughter had not lost the Falling-Leaves Moon race and disgraced his lodge. Cost him half his wealth in horses and trade goods. Clubbing her was not enough. He should have done worse. She failed him. Made him lose standing. She must now rescue him from this gods-bedamned afterworld.

He glances toward the far end of the log over the chasm where the guardian wolf beast waits. There is still a chance to cross over. Passing the pipe with his worthless daughter is key. But he is running out of patience. His thirst won't wait.

It is time for another try to draw her over the edge. He stands, curls his toes into yellow talons, spreads his black-cloaked arms into feathered wings, and flaps himself aloft. He flies toward the red-cliff edge-world, naked head glowing red in the sunlight, yellow beak clacking for a drink.

28

FALLING-DOWN WOMAN

I wake up in a willow bush, lying on my side. Something sharp presses into my eyelid. A twig. It is dark. I spit dirt out of my mouth and raise my head. Pain gallops over my left ear. I push myself up and look around. About twenty paces away the black-painted hand on Father's lodge reaches toward the moonlit sky.

The lump on the side of my head feels big as a duck's egg. I check my arms and legs, then my body. A scratch above one knee. Heels scraped, probably from being dragged. I push myself to a sitting position, then stand, testing my balance.

Little lights dance inside my head. Did Father drag me out here and throw me into this bush, like camp trash?

I stumble over to my maiden's lodge and look inside. Empty. Otter Woman's parfleche bag is gone. It dawns on me that something else is missing. I push my way back outside and realize there is empty space where her lodge used to be next to mine. All that is left is a circle of dirt, a ring of stones and remains of a fire. I shake my head. How long have I been lying in the bush? Has Father sent Otter Woman away?

Shy Bird nickers. I stroke her neck then make my unsteady way down the path toward the horse meadow. My stomach churns. I lean against a sapling to retch. I reach a pool in the spring-fed rivulet that flows through the horse meadow to the river. In the dim light, my dirty face stares back at me from the pool's surface.

A bruise purples my temple. I feel lucky to be felled by only one punch of Father's iron hand. *Was it just his hand, or his war club? If I had remained conscious, he might have continued to beat me like he beats Aunt.*

I lift the buckskin dress over my head, step out of my leggins, and lower myself into the pool's clear waters. I wash the dirt off my face, then cup the cold water on my neck, arms, legs, and body. My head-throbbing eases from gallop to slow trot.

My heart grows heavy at the loss of our father-daughter team. *What will happen now? Will I continue to race? Win back Father's favor? How can I atone for choosing to race in spite of knowing I had a sick horse? He had good reason to hit me.*

I struggle into my buckskins and walk back to my lodge to check on Shy Bird. She stands sleeping, apparently recovered. As I stare at her, my fingernails bite into my palms. The gloating smiles of Little Bear and So-chee float into my mind. There is an earlier memory as well: So-chee and Crazy Bones coyote-walking near Aunt's lodge, two sly schemers. *Did that old sorcerer put a curse on Shy Bird? Feed her some sickness potion?* Otter Woman might know, if I can find her.

What about Charges Ahead? Will his heart cool? It is one thing to court the esteemed Wind-In-Her-Hair Woman, winner of races, daughter of the mighty Ironhand. It is quite another to take up with "Falling-Down Woman" or whatever name will be thrust on me after my loss. Even if Charges Ahead still wants me, will Father now deny the marriage proposal as punishment for my failure?

These thoughts are stones in my heart. I crawl into my lodge, wrap myself in a blanket and try to sleep. I drift off then awaken with a start, sit up, shaking. I do not know how much time has passed. I close my eyes again but cannot sleep. Night has a way of turning suntime worries into monsters, flies into hornets. They buzz into my mind and keep me turning this way and that until I give up, grab a blanket and walk out into the night.

It is strangely warm for the Falling-Leaves time. The Road of Many Stars arcs through the sky above. Mother's spirit is up there, one of those tiny light-points. I will join her sometime. Maybe sooner would be better.

A low nicker from Shy Bird catches my ear. I step over to her, stroke her warm hide, wrap my arms around her neck, lean into her, and, with no one around to see, leak tears down my cheek. I swipe them away with my tongue. Shy Bird nuzzles my shaking shoulders.

After a while I sling the blanket around my

shoulders, pull up her picket rope and start down the path to the horse meadow. There she will find the forage to complete her recovery.

The dark path is so much a part of me that it guides my steps through the trees and shrubs that necklace the meadow. With each footfall, sadness spreads inside. I feel more alone than ever.

As I step into the open pasture, a form suddenly looms beside me. Shy Bird snorts; I jump, heart rattling.

"Takánsy?"

Charges Ahead. Shoulders wrapped in a blanket, head and single eagle plume silhouetted against the starlit sky. I breathe, reach out a hand.

"You are shaking. What is it?" His hands enfold mine. "I wanted to come to you after the race but was summoned to a council by our chief to divide night watch duties."

My voice comes out strangled, catching in my throat. "Shy Bird. She needs grass. She was sick, and I'm bringing her...."

His hands find my face. I wince as his fingers graze the lump above my ear.

"What is this?"

I pull away from him. "My punishment for losing the race."

"Ironhand did this?"

I nod.

He pulls me close. I press my face into his warm chest. My words waterfall out. I tell him about Shy Bird's sudden sickness, my failure to withdraw from the race, my suspicions about Crazy Bones, So-chee and Little Bear, my attempt to explain to Father, his clubbing me down. With each part of the telling my heart darkens. I fight tears, but they run down my cheeks.

I feel his hands on my shoulders, back,

arms, stroking the calm back into me. His voice soothes, a warm blanket quieting my tremors.

"You have done nothing wrong. Your horse is healing. You will heal."

I want to believe him. I tip my head back to look at his face, dim in the starlight. I follow his jaw line up to his cheek bones, compact ears, broad brow, warm eyes.

I ask the question I am afraid to ask. "Do you still want me for a wife?"

"Never more than now," he says. Then he presses his lips to neck.

I am swept into his current. I want to be carried away. Marriage rules crumble away in my exhausted mind. I press into him, feel his body tense, hear his ragged breathing.

I let go of Shy Bird, whisper, "yes" to his rising need, walk with him past the dark shapes of horses munching and pawing and snorting their night sounds. We hasten away from his sentry post, the grassy swale that opens like a gateway into the surrounding hills, and hurry up onto a nearby knoll crowned with tall firs.

There, on a mossy bed encircled by towering spruce trees, I open myself to Charges Ahead. Not once, but again and again, until, wrapped in our blankets, exhaustion drags us both into timeless sleep.

When my eyes flutter open the next morning, the first thing they see is the face of Little Bear.

29

THE RAID

My brother stands a few paces away, watching us. I am unable to stifle a cry. Charges Ahead leaps to his feet, knife in hand. When he sees Little Bear, he drops the knife, crouches to retrieve his cast-off clothes, clutches them to his body, and, stepping back, trips over my leg and falls backward with a grunt.

I grab my blanket to cover myself. I am aware of the smell of our love-making.

Little Bear's eyes, frost-cold, roam over us,

the depression our bodies have left in the moss, my shocked gaze. *He's memorizing this for the telling.*

"The Blackfeet stole some of our horses last night," he says. "They came and left through the swale you were supposed to be guarding." He backs off a step, still harvesting the scene with his eyes. A smile cracks his face. "We ride in pursuit. Will Charges Ahead join us? Or will he stay behind with his...woman?"

I clutch my blanket closer.

Little Bear's smile vanishes. He turns abruptly and stalks off.

I turn to Charges Ahead. "You were on guard duty?"

His eyes slide away. "Yes. With six others. We each had a portal to guard. Mine was where you...where I saw you with Shy Bird."

Shy Bird! Did the raiders steal her?

He jams one leg, then the other, into his leggings, jerks his breechcloth tight, dives into his tunic, grabs his knife, bow and quiver, and pushes his feet into his moccasins.

"I must go."

He hurries off, leaving me there on the ground. His eagle plume lies beside me.

I scramble to my feet, throw on my clothes and run through the circle of trees toward the horse pasture. My mind races backward, remembering the French trader's warning about a sighting of Blackfeet raiders to the South. The reason for the extra night lookouts.

The meadow is still dotted with horses. Not all are stolen. Bays, sorrels, pintos. My eyes jump here and there searching for a black with two white stockings. I force my gaze on one section of pasture at a time.

Nothing. I run along the edge of the meadow, looking behind willows and alders and the occasional hillock that might hide a horse. I call for her. There is no answering whinny.

My shoulders slump. There is nothing to do but slink back to my lodge. Hide. When I get there I duck inside. No one sees me. I hear shouts of people gathering around the chief's lodge. Buzzing wasp sounds. A chill comes over me. A dawning that is more to worry about than a stolen horse. Was anyone killed in the raid?

Why did I so easily fall into the mating-way with Charges Ahead? I wanted comfort, to be sure. It felt safe to be in his arms. But I have brought disgrace on myself and Charges Ahead.

What bad spirit possessed me? Did old Crazy Bones put a hex on me as well as on Shy Bird? My mind crow-hops for clues before the race— strange tasting food, unusual visits by birds or animals, traces of powder sprinkled on my clothes or moccasins. Nothing.

Yet some powerful medicine had overcome my own. Or perhaps it was not that powerful. *Had I not neglected my prayers, put aside my own cleansing rituals, failed to draw on the strength of my spirit-partner?* Without spiritual protection it is hard to control anger, resist temptation, dampen urges. Otter Woman often warns that in such a state, it is hard to ward off even a mild hex.

I lie down and bury my face in my buffalo robe. The weight of what I have done presses me down. I have thrown away my maidenhood, devalued myself. The whispered words of censure, spreading through the band like an evil wind, would soon reach every lodge. Little Bear would make sure of that.

What will Father do? Beat me again? Cast me out? Take a knife to my nose?

The sound of drumbeats start up from somewhere in the center of the circle of lodges. Voices buzz louder. Was someone killed during the raid? Charges Ahead will be blamed for the stolen horses. Worse if the Blackfeet murdered a lookout. His reputation will be ruined. He will be subjected to hard words, or even revenge, by the dead warrior's family. He will want to redeem himself. Risk his life in a taking-back raid. All my fault!

My heart flutters inside my chest, a caged bird. I jump up. My feet trace a quickening circle around the inside of my lodge.

I must find Otter Woman. She will know what to do.

30

WAR DANCE

I wait until sun-asleep before slipping out
of my lodge. By that time the sounds of war-
making pulse through the camp. Drum beats, the
quavering sing-song chants of warriors preparing
for battle, a steady murmur of angry voices, the pop
and crackle of fire. Above the lodge poles, from the
center of the ring of lodges, sparks dart skyward,
fade to black ash and float back toward earth like
ghosts in the moon glow. The smell of wood smoke
and sweating bodies lace the air as I draw closer.

Crouching low, I creep around the outer
lodge ring until I find Snow-Cave-Man's crude

shelter. He has moved from the horse meadow to be closer to others. To be safer. *Will Snow-Cave-Man still be a friend after learning what I have done? Does he know already?*

Staying low, I edge around his lodge and move closer to the fire. Crouching, I am aware of the soreness in my body, some from my beating and some from love-making.

Around the flames I see dancing warriors, bodies slick with sweat. Each dancer acts out his own heroic deeds in the upcoming taking-back raid. One thrusts a lance into an imaginary enemy, jerking it out with a yell. Little Bear prances as if on horseback, picking off phantom riders with rapid-fire launches of imaginary arrows. A heavyset youth plods around the circle burying his tomahawk into make-believe Blackfeet brains. Young Berry Picker brandishes his father's old black-powder weapon, one of the first acquired by the people from a Lightskin trader named Tom-son who came from cold-ward. He fires the weapon once and appears relieved that it still works. The Blackfeet, I recall with a shudder, have a big advantage when it comes to black powder weapons.

Charges Ahead lunges into view from behind the bonfire. Black paint covers the left side of his face, from hairline to throat. Red arrow symbols, dark as blood, line his upper arms. Shed of all clothing save moccasins and a red breechcloth that flaps against the hard muscles of his thighs, he thrusts a knife this way and that as his feet pound a fierce beat on the hard ground. His wild eyes cause my heart to race.

Instead of singing his own exploits, he circles around each of the other dancers, shouting encouragement, extolling their bravery, praising their warrior spirits. Is he trying to be their leader?

That is when it strikes me, the oddness of this war dance. None of the older warriors, the ones with experience, are in the circle. No Two Scalps, the customary war chief. No Crazy Bones, with his shaman bundle. He should be out there by now, invoking the spirit-partners of the fighters, praying for protection and victory and reporting on the favorable omens he conjures with his collection of bones and feathers and animal skins. Only the young warriors dance, several of them barely older than me. Boys trying to fire up their courage against the fear demons.

I drop to all fours and creep closer, trying to make myself invisible. I strain to locate Otter Woman among the circle of figures watching the dancers. *Not there.* I backtrack toward the lodge of Snow-Cave Man.

When I get there I catch the sound of his voice coming from inside. "...not wise, not wise," he is saying.

At the sound of the next voice I shrink into a crouch beside the lodge cover.

"The trail will grow cold if they wait." My father's throaty rasp.

"Better a cold than a deadly one," Snow-Cave Man says.

"The more dangerous the trail, the greater the honor to those who take it."

"True. Of course, our gimpy legs allow us to stay behind." Snow-Cave Man laughs, but there is an edge to it. "What about the owl? Old Crazy Bones said he saw it clearly, in the clouds."

Father makes his favorite snorting sound. "Crazy Bones is always seeing things."

"But would you go on a raid cursed by an owl?" Snow-Cave-Man's voice is respectful, but insistent.

"These young warriors do not put much stock in Crazy Bones' owls," Father says. "Besides, we must get my horses back."

"They weren't so many. We can raid the Snakes and get more horses. The Snakes don't have as many black-powder weapons."

"I suspect Charges Ahead is eager to get those horses back. He was supposed to be on lookout duty when the Blackfeet took them."

Snow-Cave-Man remains silent for a moment. Then he says, "Maybe he is too eager. Eagerness sometimes leads to mistakes."

"His mistake was sleeping with his breechcloth down."

At this, shame-heat rises to my face. Snow-Cave Man makes no reply.

Father's tone sharpens. "I am looking for my daughter. Has she been here?

"No. I have not seen her since the race."

"The race!" A slap of words. "She must pay for that."

"What do you plan to..."

"Banish her. I will remove her maiden's lodge from my circle. I sent the old woman away. Otter Woman cost me plenty, and with what result? A waste! Instead of keeping her virgin value, my daughter fucks the man who is supposed to guard the horses. She deserves to have her nose cut off."

Snow-Cave Man hesitates for a moment, then says, "But that punishment is for wives who betray their husbands with another..."

"Buffalo dung! She deserves that, and worse," Father spits this out like poison. "You have befriended her. If she comes to you, I expect you to tell me."

The sound of Father getting to his feet freezes me in a rabbit trance. He ducks out through the lodge entry and looms black against the fire glow in the night sky. I crouch not more than two paces away. I try to stop breathing. He looks first to one side then turns in my direction. I shut my eyes. When I open them again he is limping away toward the dancers and the fire.

I suck in a breath, stand and continue circling behind the outer ring of lodges. The image of an owl's shadow seems to hover in pursuit, growing darker with each step.

Finally I spot Otter Woman's lodge. No light flickers from within. I run the last few paces and stop in front of the open entry flap. I call to her and am answered by silence. I duck inside. With the help of light from the warrior bonfire filtering in through the lodge opening, my night eyes make out a pot of uneaten stew suspended above gray ashes in the center fire pit, bags of potions suspended from lodge poles, plants on a drying rack on one side. A smell triggers a dream-memory of my dead mother.

Then I see the still form lying on the buffalo robe at the rear.

31

SHE IS GONE

I step around the fire pit and fall to my knees beside Otter Woman. My fingers roam across the familiar creases around her cheeks and mouth. Her face is cold. No breath escapes her lips, no vein pulses in her bone-thin wrists. Her arms resist my attempt to lay them across her chest. I brush aside the strands of hair that spill across her throat and lower my ear to her chest. It is silent as stone.

Suddenly remembering Shy Bird's strange sickness, I peer closer at Otter Woman's mouth, feel it for evidence of dried greenish foam. *Nothing.*

I push up from the lodge floor, all senses alert for her spirit-being. *Is it hovering nearby, as spirits are said to do when death comes suddenly? Or when death comes from murder. The owl! Crazy Bones's owl!*

I back out of the lodge opening, feet unsteady, hands shaking.

I run back to Snow-Cave Man's lodge, burst in on him and choke out my story. His face tenses in reaction to my rude entry, but he remains calm when I tell him what I just discovered. He plucks three burning twigs from the fire, tilts them earthward to keep them alight, and hobbles after me to Otter Woman's lodge. He kindles a small blaze in her cook fire and bends over to examine the still form.

"She is gone."

"But how?" I want to know.

I rock back on my heels trying to remember when I last saw her. The trading circle, watching Upside Down Face unpack his trade goods. A few sleeps before the race. She seemed fine then. Maybe a little slow getting up. *Had she been sleeping longer than usual in the time when she shared the space next to my maiden's lodge?* I can't recall.

After my beating she was not waiting when I returned to my maiden's lodge. Was that when Father ordered her to move her lodge? I take a closer look around in the flickering firelight. There beside her pallet is her parfleche, the one with her tools, plants and medicines that had been in my lodge. She must have brought it here the previous night. Then lay down and died?

Snow-Cave Man pulls a blanket over Otter Woman's face.

"Aren't you going to…check her?" I want to know. "Shouldn't she be…was she…murdered?"

His eyes leap to meet mine.

"Why do you say this?"

In a rush of words I tell him about Shy Bird's sickness, my suspicions about my sister and brother and Crazy Bones, my fears about the old shaman's dark magic.

He reaches out with a calming hand to my shoulder. "Be at ease, granddaughter. Magic is not a part of my belief. Evil yes. But in my life I have learned that spells and hexes do not work without a little help from human hands. Poison maybe, or a shutting off of air, or a thin blade that leaves little trace. In the full light of sun-awake we will bring another medicine-woman to examine her body." He pauses, nods toward the still form. "Otter Woman was well-respected, even beloved, by many among our people. She will receive a burial worthy of her place of honor."

I fight back rising tears. My replacement mother. That is what she was for me.

But I keep this to myself and say, "She was not loved by Crazy Bones."

"True. To him she was a threat to his powers with her knowledge of plants and the ancient healing-ways. I believe our Chief will not rest without a full search for the cause of her death."

He rises from his crouch, knees cracking.

"Now we must look after you. The bruises on your face were not caused by magic."

My hand jumps to cover the lump on my head. "I do not know what to do. That is why I came to Otter Woman. Now she is gone, and I am afraid. For me and for Charges Ahead..." My voice trails off. I search his face, cling to the sympathy I see in his eyes.

"It will be best for you to be away for a while. Your father's anger is cresting high."

I tell him I overheard Father's threat to cut off my nose.

He takes my hand and leads me out of Otter Woman's lodge.

"Take some food and blankets and skins for a small shelter. Snows may come at any time, so be prepared. Is there a place you can hide?"

I tell him about the big rock meadow of my first trial quest.

"Yes, I know it. Go there and wait until I send for you. Hopefully your father's anger will cool."

I give him a grateful hug and slink off through the darkness to prepare for my flight. After a few steps I stop, return to Otter Woman's lodge, and grab her parfleche bag. A way to remember her, to keep her spirit close to me. And an idea that I may need some of the things inside.

32

SNOW-CAVE MAN

Snow-Cave Man walks along a forested alpine lakeshore in his heaven, lost in thought. The water is clear, revealing a bottom of blue, green, red and white stones near where it laps gently against the shore before deepening into azure and cobalt further out.

He loves this place. Walking here helps him think. No limp hobbles his progress. He has shape-shifted into his younger self, before losing his toes and his manhood.

He breathes in a lungful of pine-scented air and recalls the cross-over of Otter Woman. He wonders about her spirit-being. He would like to find her here in the afterworld. Speak with her about helping the ageing Takánsy, leaning against the juniper on the red-cliff ridge of the edge-world. But how? Where?

He time-journeys back to Takánsy's discovery of Otter Woman's still form. After Takánsy goes into hiding, Snow-Cave Man alerts Big Face about the old medicine-woman's crossover. The chief sends one of his wives, a woman wise in the ways of medicine herbs, to examine Otter Woman's body. Her death remains a puzzle.

After drinking some rosewater tea to ward off possible sickness, the chief's wife washes the corpse, combs and braids the gray locks, wrestles the stiffening limbs into Otter Woman's best dress, a simple buckskin garment beaded in front with otter symbols, and lays the body out on a stack of buffalo robes for viewing.

Word of Otter Woman's cross-over quickly spreads through the village. Visiting continues for five sleeps, an outpouring of grief equal to that for a chief. The old medicine-woman has touched many lives. There is no shortage of night watchers, despite the absence of any surviving members of Otter Woman's family.

Snow-Cave Man sits for two night watches, accompanied by a daughter of Little Ignácio waving a stout switch to keep him awake lest he fall into drowsiness. The watchers never leave Otter Woman's body alone, sun-time or nighttime, making sure her spirit-being is aware of how much they venerate her.

Mourners are too many to count. Black-robe followers as well as believers in the Salish-way enter and linger beside Otter Woman's body. Snow-Cave Man takes note of those few who stay away.

Not surprisingly, Crazy Bones holes up in his lodge. Ironhand is not seen, maybe weak on stagger-water. At one point, So-chee slinks in just before dusk, kneels for a few moments before leaving, eyes downcast. No Takánsy, of course. But he knows she is mourning in her hiding lodge.

A deep burial pit is dug into the frosty ground on a hill covered with service berry bushes above the river. The bottom and sides are lined with flat stones on which is spread a buffalo robe to receive the body.

When Otter Woman is lowered into her final leaving place, along with a sampling of her herbal remedies and tools, she is covered with a flat "roof" of stout branches, then a layer of earth blended into the surrounding soil. No marker is placed on this spot, but a memory marker is left on the heart of each of the many people who process in a long line to and from the hill.

As they leave, someone cries out and points to the river. There, slicing through the water's surface swims the sleek brown form of a river otter.

After the burial, the wives of Big Face begin preparations for a Feast for the Dead, when food will be served and Otter Woman's possessions will be handed out to those close to her. But before that can happen, a rider gallops into the village with news that the war party of Charges Ahead has been sighted returning from its attempt to retrieve the stolen horses.

David Jessup

Snow-Cave Man slips away from the circle of lodges to let Takánsy know. As he limps through the snow toward her hiding place, he thinks about her losses: her mother, her horse race, her Shy Bird, her honor, her father's approval, and now, her medicine-woman guide. *Will Charges Ahead be next?*

33

WARRIORS' RETURN

My mind is crumbling. There is a hole in my heart that Otter Woman filled. There is no one to share my despair. My time in hiding drags me toward a pit. I ache for news about Charges Ahead and his war party. The waiting is torture. I lose track of sleeps. I set snares for rabbits, forget to check them. I build tiny fires and let them go out. I shake with cold. I pray no one will discover my hideout.

Praying. Otter Woman's voice comes to me, awake and asleep.

"You let yourself get separated from your spirit-partner," she says. "Bad things happen when you neglect your protector spirits. They leave, and there is no one to stop the bad spirits and other people's hexes getting to you."

So I pray. I call on the horse-spirit. I pray to Amotken, the Above Being, creator and protector, the One who sends animals and plants as messengers and partners to the people. I promise I will never again fail to keep the spirits near. I promise to keep them in my heart awake and dreaming, call on them in good times and bad, promise them daily attention through ritual and cleansing. I beg them for strength, for protection. And above all, for the safe return of Charges Ahead. I pray upon awakening, three more times during sun-time, and once before falling into exhausted sleep. Surely, I hope, nothing else bad can happen after so much praying. But the death owl drifts on silent wings through the dark nights of my aloneness.

A skiff of snow blankets my shelter. Shadows lengthen toward sun-asleep. I hear the crunch of footfalls in the snow. They have come for me. I am almost glad. Punishment is due. Anything would be better than to stay in this alone world. I peer through an opening in the hide cover.

Snow-Cave Man. He limps toward me. There is no smile on his face. He squeezes into my tiny shelter, sits and pulls a piece of pemmican out of his pouch, offers It to me. I thank him but set it aside. My hunger is for news.

He tells me of the burial of Otter Woman. The outpouring of grief, the honors heaped on her. The cause of her death, still a mystery. I give up trying to hold back my tears.

He tells me the war party has been sighted a

half-sleep away. The warriors will return tomorrow. I can return to the circle of lodges with him. He says my father's anger has cooled. He says he has persuaded Ironhand to relent. The price: three of Snow-Cave Man's horses.

I turn away, clench my jaw to keep from crying again. I do not deserve this man's kindness.

Together we walk back to the village. Behind Shining Mountain a bank of clouds muscles up from the horizon, threatening to blot out the descending sun. One cloud, detached from the rest, mimics a bird with puffy wings, head outstretched toward the sun, gooselike. Or owl-like. The cloud-bird's shadow sweeps from the river across the meadow and onto the ring of lodges. Cone-shaped shadows fade and disappear. The smell of abandoned cook fires reaches my nostrils. Most lodges are empty of people.

On the far side of the circle of lodges I hear the faint padding of moccasin footfalls and the murmur of voices—subdued voices, except for an occasional child's cry—gathering to welcome back our warriors.

We pass through the far ring of lodges and come up behind a small knot of women, some with children at the breast, hurrying toward the river trail on the upstream side of the Bitterroot. The trail where Charges Ahead and the young warriors had galloped off sleeps ago—a moon ago?—in pursuit of horses and restored honor.

People are pushing into two ragged lines, a lane through which the returning riders will pass. Soon, the rear part of the passageway is clotted with impatient mothers anxious for their sons' safe return. I stretch on tiptoe to peer over their heads.

No one is shouting. The mood is somber.

I turn to Snow-Cave Man, ask him if has heard advance news.

He shakes his head no.

A cry erupts from the far end of the line.

"They come!"

The first face I see is Little Bear's. His features are stone, revealing nothing. His left shoulder is smeared with dirt. A pink welt rages across his chest from collarbone to the opposite rib. Save for the up and down rhythm of pointed ears and horse's mane moving in time with his upper body, I cannot see the horse he is riding. Between Little Bear and the next warrior rides a captured Blackfeet brave, hands trussed behind, neck encircled with two horsehair lassos, one held in the hand of Little Bear, the other by young Berry Picker, riding behind. Berry Picker's face is no-longer-boyish; his eyes have the look of someone who has seen things not meant for the young.

The prisoner appears older than his captors. Battle scarred, he looks straight ahead as he moves through the sound of angry voices that rises like an ill wind through the lines of watchers. Yellow paint bridges his nose from cheek to cheek. Blood oozes down his arm from an arrow shaft protruding from the front of his right shoulder.

My eyes quickly move from the captive to the next rider, and the next, and the next, lingering on each only long enough to note the absence of the one I seek. Then, between the last rider and the one before, a gap appears where a rider should have been. Not a gap, a riderless horse. I will myself taller, legs straining. A body lies across the horse's back. I quickly look back over the line of riders. Had I missed him? *No.*

I push people aside to reach the front of the

line, no longer caring if I am discovered. I see a gently swinging arm with a red arrow painted on it. A face painted black on one side from neck to hairline, and finally, as the horse walks past, a gaping hole in the back of his head matted dark with clotted blood ringed with jagged white bone edges spearing gobs of pink.

I fall back onto my rump and scrabble backward through the forest of knees and legs that jump aside as I scream.

34

ROCK THAT STANDS

Rock-That-Stands faces his Salish enemies, the last he will ever see. A death circle, men on the outside, women closer in. The women's eyes, how they glitter! Teeth bared like wolves. Most of the time women are caring, obedient, compassionate. But not with prisoners. Not now. With prisoners they are hungry for revenge. Blackfeet women are the same. All hurt and hatred. He can see it building in their hard, feasting eyes, the set of their mouths.

But he is ready for them. Has he not sung

his death song during the night? Sung of his horse stealing, his many coups, his courage? Rock-That-Stands, Blackfeet warrior. His people will tell his story for many winters. His children and his grandchildren will tell it. He pictures his youngest grandson for a moment, eager smile, dark eyes full of pride. Then he bans the image. Not something he can afford to dwell on at this moment. He must focus his entire being on what is about to happen.

Has he not prayed for strength? Strength against the pain that is coming. Strength to laugh at it, to fling it back in their faces. His will be a death without shame. A death his enemies will remember. The kind of death that will add to their defeat, rob them of any heart-help in his capture. A quick death, with no shameful outcries.

He has imagined what they will do to him. Jabs, cuts, burns, gouges. Rehearsed his response. Rubbed the arrow shaft in his shoulder against the ground to test his resistance to pain. Practiced separating himself from the pain, as he and his friends have done since they were young. Learned to build a wall between the pain and his tongue, so as not to let a scream out of his mouth. Taught himself to laugh instead. Last night he managed to laugh while twisting the arrow. He will laugh today.

He will also taunt. He knows some Salish words learned from captured Flathead slave girls. One of them he has lain with; liked, even. She has unwittingly prepared him for this moment. Helped him know how to pick out the weak ones. Practice the words he will say to the enemy women, the reactions in their faces that will give them away.

He searches his memory again for Flathead prisoners they have taken—their capture, their weaknesses. Of their torture and death, he makes up unflattering images and practices the words to tell about them.

Then there is the battle itself, fresh in his mind. The black painted half-face who rode fearlessly into their ranks, not once, but twice, so close that Rock-That-Stands' head-shot was easy. His large-bore musket ball had blasted a hole in the enemy rider's head. Then the milling confusion of the other Flatheads after their leader fell. Their retreat in a shower of bullets. His own hot pursuit of them, closing in.

Then the cursed badger hole, his bad luck. He remembers hearing the snap of his horse's foreleg. Remembers flying through the air, then blackness. Too bad the tree limb or rock or whatever had struck his head did not finish him off. Instead, these young warrior pups captured him without a fight. Got ropes on him before he came to. Hidden him well, the cowards, avoiding discovery by his own warriors' search party.

All this he will turn to his advantage. His eyes probe the circle of angry faces, looking for those with the most fury. Those likely to lose control.

The woman waving a skinning knife. Hard eyes. She will flay me limb by limb. No help there. But the tall long-hair beside her—the braidless one. A possibility. Her eyes look haunted—strange gray eyes. Like she has suffered a loss. Maybe she has. Maybe the one I shot.

What about that short one there, is he not the one who led me here with a rope around my neck? Yes, that is him. Stocky little shit-dog. Worth a try. Calm, though. Looks just like the older one by his side, the one with the bad leg. Leave that one alone—nothing but hardness there.

What about that young one with the topknot? A wish-he-were-warrior, unsure. And he has a knife. Knives are better than those sticks with fire.

I start my goading-talk. "You, topknot head. Feeling brave now? Think you can stick me now I tied up? Or you are shake like aspen leaf, like when you fight?"

That gets to him! His face goes red, his knuckles white on his knife. And his eyes! Alarm and fear. Good!

"Come on, come on, or are you still boy."

He comes toward me. Good. But what's this? Stocky boy pushes Topknot aside, steps in front, eyes me, lifts knife, cuts under my fingernails, one by one. Slow. Must laugh.

"Ha Ha. You not hiding now, short boy, not afraid anymore, like in battle. You fat squaw! You should have name 'Hides-in-Bushes...*Uhh*."

His knee in my man parts. I did not see that coming. Must watch better—no more surprises, no more crying out. Only laughing.

"Ha ha! Hides-in-bushes."

Knife at my stomach now, slicing. Good. Not much pain, lots of blood. More blood, the better.

"Ha Ha."

These cursed leather thongs! Cutting my wrists. Keeping my arms up pinned to tree. Cannot protect myself. Cannot double over. Spirit Above, how my body wants to double over! Better I remain upright, against this tree. Rock-That-Stands; Death-That-Stands. Must get someone else, though. That woman. There! Hatred flaring. Maybe the Mother.

"You remember Flathead girl we take last winter, pretty one missing toe and big breasts? You want hear what happen to her?"

Her hate eyes on mine, where I want them.

"Her name now 'Spreads-Her-Legs.' Every

Blackfeet man fucks her. We poke her until she bleed. Ha ha ha."

Running at me, yes, yes, come on, come on, blade flashing, yes, there goes my cock, yes, much bleeding now. And here comes another—I get them moving, voices rumbling, anger flowing, almost out of control. Here's another—knife to ears, no ears now, blood in place of ears. Good! Burning brand into armpit hurts!

"*Unnhh*. Ha Ha."

Oh no, woman, not my eyes, my goading-way, you will not get them out.

The circle closes in. Yes! Keep coming! Blows, stabs, firebrands. Harder to see now. Harder to prepare for blows. Oh Gods, there goes my stomach. Ripped open. My guts hanging out, brushing the ground. Oh Gods Oh Gods Oh Gods how it hurts! Must not pass out!

"*Uhhhhhnnnnngggg*."

They back away, staring at my guts. *Don't stop now, don't stop, don't stop. Spirit help, Spirit help, don't stop! Where is ghost-eye woman? There she is.*

"Black...half-face...man...stupid! I kill him easy! Not brave...STUPID! Not warrior...FOOL! Not..."

Yes, Here comes Ghost-Eye running at me, long hair flying, hatchet upraised. Yes, yes, hurry! Hands reach to stop her, pull her back, voices shouting, 'Not yours...' and 'Your fault...' and 'Slut bitch...' and 'Stop her...'

"Let her come let her come let her come."

Her animal shriek clears a path. She rushes forward, lifts her hatchet, and ...a flash, blackness, and no more pain.

35

OBSIDIAN

Where does one go when the unthinkable happens? To whom does one turn? Not to my horse-spirit. Guardian spirits can help you, even protect you, if you pay them homage, learn from them, call on their medicine. But I am beyond help. I need something different from medicine. I need something for the pain in my heart. Something spirit-partners cannot give.

I open Otter Woman's parfleche and rummage through the dried plants and powder pouches and healing potions. My hand finds what

I'm looking for. A chunk of obsidian, shiny black along its thick side, see-through gray on its thin edge, so thin I can see the buckskin beneath it. The same blade Otter Woman used to shave roots for my love charm.

Sharper than any knife, I pick it up with care. Its thick side settles comfortably into my palm. I move it up and down, feeling its weight. It feels right for what I have in mind. My index finger curls around one end and finds a flat surface that feels molded to fit. Its cutting edge faces outward. With a flick of my wrist, I snick off a strand of leather fringe from my shirt.

You won't feel a thing, I say to myself.

My eyes tear. I have done more crying during the past sleeps than during all my winters. We are not supposed to cry like this. Wailing, yes, the kind you are supposed to do when you lose a parent or husband. Or child. But not these long, moaning, rib-squeezing sobs that leave me gasping, head down, barely able to sit up straight, fighting for the next breath, the kind that steal your dignity and brand you as weak, the kind you only do in private. It feels as though a river has been flowing through my body and out through my eyes.

The hatchet blade I buried in the Blackfeet prisoner's forehead should have been sunk into my own—would have been, if Snow-Cave Man had not stopped me. The parents of Charges-Ahead might have finished the job, such was their fury. Robbed first of their son, then of their right of revenge by watching his killer suffer.

But ending the enemy's suffering was not my intent. Hatred drove me forward; hatred of the Blackfeet's face, which, in the moment of striking, I remember with a shudder, became my own.

The prisoner fired the bullet that killed

Charges Ahead. But I was the one who sent him into danger. The suffering I tried to end with the hatchet blade was my own.

That was six sleeps ago. A time of crying and, despite Snow-Cave Man's best efforts, a time of barely eating. Father has not come for me to whip me or punish me. My punishment is shunning and banishment. Worse than losing a nose. But their opinion of me, low as it must be, cannot be as low as my own.

I duck into my hiding lodge, sit on my sleeping robe and take the glassy stone out of its pouch. It seems to glow as twilight descends. I reach for my throat, probing. My fingers find the blood pulse there. One quick stroke will do it. Death will come quickly.

Snow-Cave Man will find me in the morning. He will be disappointed in me. I wish he would not be the one to discover my body. He will pray to Jésu for my departed spirit, or *soul* as he calls it. But I am not destined for his heaven. Not after what I have done.

Nor will I enter the Great Beyond to find Otter Woman. I will never make it across the log spanning the river between worlds. I will not be allowed. My spirit will hover close by for a season or more, frightening any who stumble upon my hiding lodge. I will take the form of owl, ghost-winging through the night. Then I will go where? Into nothingness?

I cannot think of a single person other than Snow-Cave Man who will lament my crossover. Most will consider it just. So-chee may go through the motions of mourning, but she will not mean it. Aunt will flutter and keen a short-lived lament. Little Bear? He will be glad to be rid of me.

And Father? I have not seen him since

the race. He does not even try to find me. Snow-Cave Man tells me the family of Charges Ahead is demanding a payment from him to make up for the loss of their son. His horse and betting losses leave him with little to give. Now he is falling prey to the stagger-water. Taos Lightning, it is called. The foul-tasting liquid, poured out from little wooden casks by Lightskin traders, does strange things to people.

Snow-Cave Man tells me the Lightskins trade the stagger-water in return for pelts, especially beaver. He says my father is too proud to get his feet wet in the beaver ponds, so he pays others to collect the furs. He pays them with horses. His herd grows smaller. After the Blackfeet raid, Father sent a nephew out to a trading post near Canyon Gate to bring back one of the casks. For the next two sleeps he was staggering about, cursing, and sometimes falling. Hitting his wives. Snow-Cave Man says that Aunt has new bruise marks on her arms and neck, and around her right eye.

One more reason to depart this world. I won't have to go back to that. I won't have to remember that I helped cause his downfall. I look down at the obsidian blade. It is time.

I pick up the obsidian. Its cutting edge catches the fading light. With my other hand I grab my chin and pull it up. I lean forward, positioning my throat over the edge of the sleeping robe. I set the blade back down and begin my death song. It comes out in a hoarse moan. Not the clear, strong tones I want.

> *Gone am I*
> *Gone am I*
> *To the land beyond the waters.*

To the dark land that sees no sun.
To the bottom-of-the-world land
that sees no joy.
Here will I spend my spirit life.
Takánsy, daughter of Ironhand.
Here will I spend my spirit life.

My upper body starts to sway in rhythm to the song's beat.

I will be no more.
No one will join me there.
No one will sing my song.
I will be no more.
I sing goodbye to Charges Ahead
I sing goodbye to Otter Woman
I sing goodbye to Snow-Cave-Man
I sing goodbye to Shy Bird.
I sing goodbye to the horse-spirit,
The horse-spirit that I have forsaken.
Better there than this world.
Better there than this world.
Better there...

Snow-Cave Man bursts into my lodge, nearly overturning it in his haste. He must have heard my song. I did not hear his approach.

His eyes travel between the black stone and my face, then back again.

"Oh, my poor Takánsy," he says. He sets his cane aside and lowers himself next to me. Picks up the stone and sets it aside. Reaches toward me and draws me close.

"No. No. No." I push against him, but I am too weak to resist. I am enfolded. Rocked in his arms like a child.

After a while he says, "You are forgiven."

I shake my head. "You can forgive me all you want. It makes no difference."

"Not me. I am not talking about me."

I pull back and gape at him.

"Jésu. Jésu forgives you. He has forgiven others who have done far worse than you."

"No one has done worse than me."

"Hush." He cuts me off with an impatient wave of his hand. "Takánsy, granddaughter, listen well. You think you should have the power to end your life, but you are wrong. That power belongs only to God, to Amotken." He pauses, then adds, "You are like a child who thinks only of herself."

"Yes, that is what caused...everything."

"So why do you keep doing it?"

This causes me to stop and think. Ending my life is selfish? It does not seem so to me.

He taps my forehead with his finger, forcing my eyes to meet his.

"Jésu says that anyone can change and be forgiven. Anyone. I know a man who did something far worse than you. He fell in love with another man's wife. He schemed for a way to get rid of the woman's husband. Then came a time when he saw his chance. He found out the husband was planning a trip. A trip to a Lightskin trading post. The man sent word to an enemy tribe. They would set an ambush, he knew. He was right. The only problem was that just before he left, the husband decided to take his family with him. Just a whim."

Snow-Cave-Man draws a long breath. He has my full attention.

"The whole family was murdered. The wife. Two children. Everyone."

My breath catches.

"The man—the one who had schemed—

knew his life was destroyed. No one else knew what he had done, but he couldn't bear the shame of it. He began preparing his death song. To die by his own hand. Then something happened. A miracle."

"What miracle?"

"As he fasted and prepared for death, the man had a vision. In the vision, Jésu appeared. He looked just like the man in the Black-robe pictures. Jésu looked at the man with big kind eyes. Eyes that asked...*demanded*...him to live. Jésu said, 'Walk in my path, and you will be forgiven.' Just that. He kept repeating it. 'Walk in my path, and you will be forgiven.'

"The man abandoned his death song and went to the Black-robes for help. He wanted to know about the Jésu path. The Black-robes took him in. They taught him all about the Black-robe-way. And in the end, the man was saved from death."

Snow-Cave-Man takes hold of both my shoulders.

"Takánsy, you must not do anything until you talk with this man. He is Little Ignácio."

"Little Ignácio. The man who brought the Black-robe?"

"Yes."

I feel the tears beginning to flow. I thought there could not be any left. I reach out, clutch his sleeve and collapse onto his folded knees. For long minutes I sob as he pats me with his big calloused hands and awkward murmurs.

Then he rises, pulls me to my feet and says, "It is time to return to your maiden's lodge."

I look down at the obsidian blade, inert and black against the sleeping robe. I turn and walk beside Snow-Cave-Man into the night, holding onto his big hand like a lost child.

36

THE VOW

Forgive the terrible wrong. Take away the shame. Love the pariah. No spirit-partner has this power. Only Jésu. And he is using it for me. To save me.

Little Ignácio tells me these things as he and Snow-Cave Man comfort me in the warmth of Ignácio's wife's lodge. I lap up his words like a thirsty puppy. Ignácio's wife brings me food. Bundles me in robes. Sponges my dirty face with soft doeskin soaked in warm water. Strikes a spark of life in my wasted body.

Having a new spirit-partner that cares about me, that loves me enough to forgive my great sin, is for me a floating log in a raging river, something to grab and hold onto to stop from drowning.

Others follow the Black-robe-way for different reasons. They seek medicine to protect them from Blackfeet raids, from sickness and hunger. From storms, from cowardice, from humiliation. They want medicine to help them win races, get rich, attract a lover, defeat enemies.

I want protection from myself. Medicine to stop me from doing bad things. To keep me alive when bad things happen to me. Jésu gives me a way to keep living.

I ask Snow-Cave Man about Otter Woman. He tells me her crossover is still a mystery. No marks on her body. No sign of potions or poisons. Old Crazy Bones never left the war dance circle on the night of her crossover. So-chee was with First Wife the whole night. Little Bear was with the young braves and left the next sun-time to chase the Blackfeet raiders.

I sigh. How I miss Otter Woman. Her eye-winks, two-tooth smiles, knobby hands and wrinkled hide. Her wisdom. My guide, my teacher. My missing mother.

My own standing with the people is uncertain, Snow-Cave Man says. I am under the protection of Little Ignácio's lodge, with the agreement of Big Face. But many, including some Jésu followers, are not accepting my return.

The family of Charges Ahead is still hot with anger. They have gotten all they can out of Father, whose standing has fallen to the bottom. As for me, they call for me to be sent away, no more part of our band. Others are not so hard in their hearts. Shunning is enough, they say. I am not sure which sounds worse.

Over the next few sleeps I am taught a Jésu song to sing when the Black-robe followers gather for their seventh-day ceremony. I am given a small cross made of silver to hang around my neck. It warms against my skin when I tuck it inside my shirt. A beautiful thing, full of great medicine. I learn prayer words to say while touching a string of black beads, a *rosary*, they call it. I do the touching sign.

I am well along the healing road, but not yet to the end. What remains is my act of *atonement*. This Black-robe word, Little Ignácio tells me, means something I must do to pay for my sin. Something I must give up. I think about this as I recover. Pray on it.

One night it comes to me, what I must do. I lay aside my sleeping robe and quietly pull on my moccasins and clothes. The lodge fire glow is almost out. Soft breathing sounds from sleeping forms in the Ignácio lodge. I wrap myself in a blanket and creep out into the darkness.

Snow and stars light the way out from the circle of lodges to my hiding lodge in the big rock meadow. I brush the snow off the entry flap and crawl in. My hands grope for the parfleche, then roam over the robe I left there, then close on Otter Woman's obsidian blade, staying clear of its cutting edge. From my shirt I draw forth the silver cross and hold it before me, barely visible in the dark shelter.

I sing the Black-robe song-prayer I have learned, make the touching sign, and make my vow into the cold emptiness:

Jésu, my sins are mountains,
Casting dark shadows on my life.
The shadow of my lover's death.
The shadow of my father's fall.
The shadow of my loss of honor.
The mountains of pride, of jealousy,
of spirit neglect,
Only you, Jésu, can level these mountains,
Shine your light into these shadows,
Save my life.
For this I give you my thanks,
And make this vow of atonement:
Never more shall I ride the racing-way,
Never more feel the wind in my hair
from the back of a running horse,
Never more have the joy of race-winning
in my heart,
Never more seek standing among the people
for my way with horses.
This vow I seal with a mark
to be always with me,
To never forget.

I return the cross to its resting place around my neck. My fingers are stiff with cold. I shrug the blanket off my shoulders and pull off my shirt. Cold bumps rise on my bare skin. I pick up the obsidian blade with its rounded edge in my left hand and press it into the flesh of my upper right arm, just below the shoulder. The blade is so sharp I scarcely feel it. But there is no mistaking the hot trickle down my arm, black against my skin, and the smell of fresh blood. Atonement blood.

The scar will remain with me as a forever reminder to not walk the self-seeker path again. To sin no more.

One night I hear father howling, like a wolf. The eerie sound carries over to my maiden's lodge where I have spent the last three sleeps after leaving the Ignácio lodge. The hairs on my arms stand up like dog hackles. I peer out of the entry flap into the moonless night. A figure runs toward me.

It is Aunt. "Ironhand demands you come."

The summons, delivered through teeth clacking with cold, causes a skip in my heartbeat. I touch the cross around my neck and do the touching sign.

"Takánsy, did you hear? Hurry! He will beat us all." Aunt leans closer. Ice crystals rim her nose openings. Cloudy puffs of exhaled air frame her face. Wrinkles fan the corners of her eyes. A dark bruise clouds her left cheek.

"What does he want?"

"I do not know. He is in First Wife's lodge with that hairy-faced Papín. He caught me as I walked by and ordered me to come get you."

"Are they drinking the stagger-water?"

Aunt's worried glance backward answers my question.

"I will come." I rise.

Aunt's eyes shift to the silver cross in my hand. She touches her cheek.

"Hurry," she urges, and retreats back toward the inner circle of lodges, clutching her blanket.

Firelight flickers behind the black painted hand on the side of First Wife's lodge. I announce my arrival, voice quavering. Another wolf howl sounds from inside, followed by laughter.

I touch my nose, wondering if it will remain on my face. I should not have come. I should have found Snow-Cave Man first. I back away as the flap of the lodge opening is lifted.

Papín's hairless head appears. A white grin forms in the trimmed hair around his mouth. He beckons me forward as Father's raspy voice commands, "Enter."

Father sits at the rear of the lodge in a stained buckskin shirt. He lifts his hand to wave me in. In his other hand is a dark bottle which he raises to his lips and tips back for a long drink. The inside of the lodge looks as though it were picked clean by marauding Blackfeet. Gone are the fine garments so painstakingly made by Aunt and So-chee. Gone are most of the weapons and trophies of war that were Father's pride. Gone are the blankets and furs for trading. In their place are the remains of picked over meals, a few pouches, a blackened pot, the bedding robes, and, next to Father, a wooden cask.

The smell is of unwashed bodies, decaying food, and something new to me, a clinging, sour berry odor that must be stagger-water. The strength of it on Father's breath nearly sends me reeling.

"Sit," he says, pointing to a spot next to Papín.

I sit, confused. Instead of arrow eyes and anger face, I see eyes rimmed in red and a mouth gaping in slack-jawed mirth.

Father waves the bottle unsteadily at the two of us and says, "Daughter, Meet your new husband."

37

Red-Cliff Ridge

A rumble of thunder over the red-cliff ridge snaps me out of my mind-journey. I have been so lost in re-walking my young-woman path that I have lost track of time. A dark cloud looms over the mountains, blocking the last rays of Sun as it travels toward sun-asleep.

I glance around. No gray jay. No broken-antler deer. Time to leave red-cliff ridge. I try to push away from the juniper tree. My ageing legs have gone numb. I roll onto all fours and crawl a few paces up slope. My legs begin to tingle, and finally, after much strain, I manage to haul myself to my feet. Dizziness nearly topples me, but I lower my head enough to regain balance.

I wonder if Lena has heard me, received my mind-thoughts. My strength is waning, but I can't leave this place without trying one last time to make contact. Step by slow step I work my way upslope to where I saw her spirit-being. *Was it only a dream, a mind trick?* I find the place and call out. No answer.

I think back on my mind-journey. I have spoken, or thought, the story of my early life, a story I never wanted to remember, but which needed telling. Hoping it would help me find my Lena in the afterlife.

The rest of my story, Lena already knows. How I married Papín, who turned out to be a good man, the father of Louie Papa, Lena's half-brother. How Papín became friends with Medina, how I came to have the love-feeling for Medina, and how I was traded to Medina because I would not go with Papín to live with his people in Saint Louis. How I kept my vow to give up the horse racing-way. How I kept on the Jésu road in spite of losing my children, one by one.

Jésu helped me get through the pain of leaving my people and losing my children. Medicine to understand that suffering such losses is part of atonement. Punishments well deserved. For thirty winters I have stayed alive through many bad things. I have cut my arm with the obsidian, but never my throat. The scars remind me of my vows, of Jésu's love.

And it worked. Up until my Lena's crossover.

That was too much. That was more than I could bear. More punishment than anyone deserves. That was when Jésu turned into an evil spirit for me. No longer loving. No longer forgiving.

That is when I flung my rosary against the wall. Smashed the cross that gave me peace. Stole Lena's body so Medina could not bury her in his Black-robe cemetery. Brought her stiff and cold to this lonely ridge and hid her in this leaving place.

Here I wait. Wanting crossover, but afraid my spirit will never find hers. Afraid I will go to the Black-robe fire that never ends. Or the empty place of lost Salish spirits. Or blocked from crossing the chasm bridge that leads to the Road of Many Stars in the Great Beyond.

I no longer know what medicine to believe.

38

THE CROSSING

I am back at Mariano's Crossing, standing in the courtyard. Lena's spirit-being did not come again on the red-cliff ridge. I do not know if she has heard my story. Or if she did, whether it has made any difference. I do not know whether I am lost, or she is lost. I am losing hope that I will ever go to be with my Lena.

The sun is fading toward sun-asleep. All around me the strange purple light pulses. It throbs like a beating heart around the door on

Medina's barn. Horses mill about the corral, each outlined with an aura of glowing purple. Their tails lift, as if they sense a storm brewing, although no clouds darken the sky and no breeze stirs the cottonwoods along the river. Perhaps a stagecoach is approaching, the evening run from Denver City. The log cabins on the far side of the courtyard stand ready to receive its passengers for the night.

A lamp flickers on inside the tavern, its glow spilling out across the wood porch as Juan the bartender opens the door to peer out into the courtyard. If he is surprised to see me he does not show it. His eyes pass over me without stopping. I catch the scent of wood smoke and meat cooking on the fire pit behind the tavern, fat dripping on hot coals. Juan closes the door behind him and clomps purposefully around the corner of the tavern clutching a pan and long-handled fork.

I turn and head toward our home at the back of the trading post. Its familiar whitewashed walls catch what remains of the fading light. I step onto the porch to the back door that leads to the kitchen. I twist the door handle, ease it open, and stop dead still.

The room beyond the kitchen is full of people. There is Frank Bartholf and his wife. My oldest son, Louie Papa, looking uncomfortable in his dress-up clothes. William Alexander, white beard aquiver, with his hand on the shoulder of son John, the boy who tried to get my Lena to run away with him. My husband, Medina, stands next to that woman he fancies, Susan Howard. I catch a whiff of his pipe tobacco and her sick-sweet perfume. Father Machebeuf, hands folded in front of his robe, looking grave. Why is he here, all the way from Denver City?

They all look somber. There are no smiles, no laughter, no joking or slapping of backs. Their voices are subdued. They stand in a rough semicircle, their backs to me, facing the wall of the big room where my sleeping pad lies next to where my Jésu altar used to be, before I destroyed it. The air smells faintly of decay. I move forward to see what it is that draws their attention. Medina steps in front of me, blocking my way.

I whisper his name, but he ignores me.

"Let me pass," I say louder, but neither he nor the Howard woman turn toward me. I reach out with my hand to push them apart. Instead of his buckskin jacket and her calico blouse, my hand touches...nothing.

Fear rises like muddy floodwater in my throat. I push forward—through?—the semicircle of people to view the thing lying on my sleeping pad.

A body, dressed in one of my white-beaded doeskin dresses, arms crossed over her chest, withered hands clutching a rosary. A gray face rimmed in still black hair, high cheekbones prominent against hollowed out cheeks, lips slightly parted, eyelids held closed with brass coins to hide ghost eyes.

My eyes.

I let out a shriek that no one hears. Suddenly I am looking down on myself, on the tops of people's heads, on their hats, on their shoes and boots and moccasins pointing toward my dead body. I hover there for a long moment as comprehension dawns, then I am out through the roof, looking down on the darkening outlines of Mariano's Crossing, the receding landscape, an owl's-eye view of the stage rolling in from the south, the river snaking away to the east, rising faster and faster toward the stars and some purple light that glows ever brighter, ever more blinding.

I shut my eyes and await my fate.

39

THE DESERT

A wave of heat slaps my face. I open my eyes. I am standing in a vast expanse of barren sandy ground, sparsely populated by strange spiny desert plants. I recognize an oversized version of prickly pear, but the others are new to me: tangled ones with twisted spiny branches, tall ones with angled arms like lookouts, large round ones with vertical ribs, upended like pots drained of water.

There are no streams. Not even a patch of deep green that might signal the presence of a spring. All is gray-brown and yellow-brown. The smell of dust.

My tongue sticks to the roof of my mouth. I blink to moisten my eyes. The inner surface of my nose goes dry with each breath. The breeze brings no scent of earth or of growing things. If dry has an odor, this is it.

No sounds either. No chirp of birds, no hum of insects, no rustle of scurrying rodents. Just the occasional low moan of air stirring through cactus spines.

I try to pinch myself awake. *Can it be that I have crossed over? Am I alone in some dry, deserted afterworld?*

Heat waves shimmer from the top of a boulder as big as Medina's tavern. I make my way toward the shade on the far side. Rounding the corner, I stop, heart thumping.

A figure sits on the ground, back against the boulder. It looks at me, a familiar smile growing on its face. It rises, steps toward me, holding out a hand. It has the parched dry smell of something long dead.

"I have been hoping you would come."

I know that raspy voice. "Father?"

"Yes. Come closer. It has been such a long time." He reaches for my hand, pulls me into the shadow of the boulder and sits me down facing him, his back against the stone.

I look at him with open mouth. No sign of the shape-shifting vulture I saw earlier. His face is gaunt, his body shrivel-thin. Not much older than when I last saw him, but ravaged, as if by some disease. He wears a frayed loincloth, a belt with a knife, a worn, loose-fitting cloth shirt, a black cape thrown over his shoulders. His breath smells of rotting teeth.

His walking stick leans against the boulder, next to a collapsed water skin. No bow and arrows or black powder weapon in sight. Only his war club, and a scatter of white bones littering the ground around us.

"What happened to you?" I ask.

"Crossed over. Same as you, only much longer ago. After I sold you to Papín and you left the Bitterroot." His face twists into an angry scowl. "Fell and hit my head on a rock by the river. My wives were slow to look for me, bring me back to my lodge for medicine healing. I froze. Lazy bitches."

I do not ask what caused the fall. "Where are we?"

"In-between-world." He frowns, looks around. "A terrible place."

Are you...are we alone?" I ask.

"Yes. But if you help me, we can both leave."

"I want to go to my Lena. Do you know where she is? In a dream I had, you said you knew..."

"She is in the Great Beyond. We can join her there when we get across that." He points to a cleft in the flat expanse. A thin break winding through the flat landscape, a crack in the sunbaked surface. From this location it is nearly invisible.

I start to rise.

He grabs my arm, pulls me back down. "You will not succeed. I have tried. The crossover log is guarded by the wolf-beast. He says we must pass the pipe together before we can go."

"Pass the pipe?"

"Restore peace between us. Say we are sorry for misdeeds." He pulls a white bone from the ground and waves it in front of me. "I have no pipe, but we can make pretend with this."

He lifts one end of the bone—it looks like the leg bone of a dog or small fox—and brings it to his lips, mimicking blowing smoke. This he repeats three more times, swiveling around to face sun-awake, cold-ward and sun-asleep. The ancient ritual that precedes any important discussion, any honest exchange of heart-talk.

I stare at him. I want this to happen. The pull of my Father is still there after all these years. I recall training horses together, winning races for him, earning his confidence, becoming part of his trust-circle. Holding a place of honor in his family despite not having a mother.

But I also remember the lost race, the beating afterward. I know I deserved a beating for failing to pull Shy Bird out of the race. But Father struck me down before I was able to tell him about Shy Bird's sudden sickness, the spell cast by old Crazy Bones, my suspicions of So-chee and Little Bear. Now, here in this forsaken afterworld, I have my chance.

He hands the bone to me. I pretend to smoke, pray to the four directions. Hope kindles in my heart as I prepare to tell him my story. How to begin? I start by begging his pardon for the lost race.

He nods, frowns. "You caused me to lose much. Then the dishonor you brought on my lodge, our family, with your whoring. The death of Charges Ahead. His family turned on me because of you."

I look down. Our knees are almost touching, but the distance between us feels like a chasm. With sinking heart I try again.

"Shy Bird was sick from a spell, or poison. It was so sudden. There was no time to..."

"No excuses! You claimed to be a horse healer. You should have known."

I blunder on. "I believe Crazy Bones made a potion for So-Chee and Little Bear to give to Shy Bird."

"Why was I not told?"

"I wanted to, tried to, but you hit me, threw me out of..."

"You deserved it! I should have cut off your nose! You were worse than your mother. Yet you got off easier than her."

I am stunned. *Why bring up my mother?*

"Father, I tried my best to please you, to bring you honor. Please let us..."

"Enough! You have apologized. We have passed the pipe. Now let us go to the crossing log and see if the gods-cursed guardian wolf will let me get away from this gods-bedamned place."

I look at him. His face is stone.

He pushes himself to his feet, grabs his war club and limps off toward the chasm.

Putting things right with Father is like sand sifting through fingers. Is this the Black-robe Hell? There is no eternal fire, only constant dry heat, never-ending thirst. A land of forever punishment. Will I spend the rest of time here, alone with a Father who will not...*will never*, hear me?

Father is moving faster now, his walking stick a blur.

I struggle to my feet. He will leave without me. Leave me behind! I try to run on my wobbly legs, sand slowing me down, sucking at my feet. Up ahead, Father stops at the edge of the cleft in the desert crust.

I catch up to him, panting, and peer over the edge. Sheer rock walls plunge down into a dark abyss that seems to have no bottom. A huge log stretches across the void. Tendrils of sulfurous vapor waft up around it.

On the other side two figures materialize and walk, or float, toward us. I look with wide eyes, disbelieving.

Snow-Cave Man. Otter Woman!

Father steps back from the end of the log as they advance.

My knees go weak. I reach for something to steady myself. Snow-Cave Man floats past Father and takes hold of my elbow, eases me over to a flat stone and helps me sit. His touch is warm, firm. He limps and smiles his lop-sided smile. He is as real as the night he saved me from the Obsidian blade.

Otter Woman is first to speak. She kneels beside me, takes my other hand.

"Welcome, granddaughter. We have been expecting you." Her smile melts my heart. She looks much as she did the night before I found her body in her lodge. Shrewd black eyes in a wrinkled crone face, playful, otter smart, full of practical wisdom.

"Where are we?" I ask. "What is this place?

"Edgeworld," she says. "Purgatory," Snow-Cave Man says. They look at each other and smile, as if sharing a long-unresolved disagreement.

Behind them, Father steps onto the log. Before he can take a step, he is rocked back by some invisible force. He sprawls, stick flying, at the feet of the two spirit-beings.

"Fuck dog!" he yells, picking himself up. He turns to Snow-Cave Man. "How do you cross?" he rasps. "Tell me!"

Snow-Cave Man gives him a smile which radiates kindness, understanding.

Father does not take it that way.

"Laugh at me, you lop-sided dog face, and I will throw you into that pit." He clenches his fists, makes his arrow eyes.

Snow-Cave Man holds his ground.

"Peace be upon you, Ironhand," he says. "Peace. That is the only way to cross over."

"You sound like that cursed wolf-beast over there." He nods toward the other side of the chasm. "Pass the pipe, pass the pipe. That is all it says, over and over. Pass the fucking pipe."

"So why don't you?" Otter Woman asks, stepping closer, a bemused smile on her face.

"I did that, with daughter here, just now!" His face rages red.

"But you passed the pipe with gestures, not with heart," Snow-Cave Man says gently.

Father raises his war club, and before I can scream 'no,' swings a lethal blow at Snow-Cave Man. It passes right through the still-smiling figure and, meeting no resistance, throws Father off balance, sending him sprawling to the ground.

Otter Woman raises her hand.

"That club will do you no good against us. And another thing. There are others with whom you must pass the pipe before crossing over." She points across the gorge to the opposite end of the log, where another figure materializes. Shrouded in a white cloak, the spirit-being drifts toward us, moving across, but not touching, the log. All eyes fix on the figure's features as they slowly become visible.

A young woman, slender and beautiful, with black braided hair. She smiles. Her wide-set dark eyes fix on me. Welcoming, loving eyes.

I am transfixed. I feel like flinging myself into her arms.

"Who are you?"

"Oh my Takánsy, my little girl. Long have I waited for this moment. I am your mother."

I am struck dumb. She reaches toward me,

hand caressing my face, touch soft and warm. I am a little girl again, and I am sobbing, grasping at her hand, pulling myself against her soft body, her breasts. Her lips on my forehead, crooning some song that stirs a memory, a faint whisper from deep inside my heart.

A harsh cry draws our eyes toward Father. He scrambles to his feet. His face ashen, his eyes agog, a look of pure terror twisting his face. He staggers back, drops his war club, turns and flees toward the boulder where I first saw him, stumbling without his cane, crawling on all fours, a fear-filled, pathetic shadow of a man.

Otter Woman shakes her head. "No change in him."

Snow-Cave Man says, "He will be here a long time, I fear."

"Once he had honor, when he first courted me." Mother says, her voice low.

We turn to her.

"A brave warrior. But undone by greed, caring only for himself. Possessed by fury he would not control." Her face is sad, wistful.

I reach for her. "Mother, your crossover has haunted me all my life. My birthing. I was to blame." I bury my face in her stomach, and the sobs start again. "I missed you so much. How I wanted my mother!"

She pulls me to my feet and cups my chin in her hand to look into my eyes. "He told you that?"

"Yes. That I was too big. I am so sorry."

She gives my shoulders a little shake. "My poor child. That is not true." She turns to Otter Woman. "Tell her."

Otter Woman nods. "You slid out of your mother's birthing tunnel easy as a river otter slips down its slide. I almost did not have time to catch you before you hit the ground." She cackles at the memory, flashing her two-toothed smile. "You were long in the leg, but skinny."

My mind swims, revisiting memories that swirl with new meanings. "But Mother, if I was not to blame, then who...what caused...?

"My crossover?" She turns to point at the war club Father dropped on the ground. The massive gray river stone is cradled in the curved fork of an ironwood branch, strapped in place by strands of dried sinew. "That. Smashed my head in while I was recovering in the birthing lodge."

"But why?"

"Jealous rage. He saw your gray eyes. The same color as the eyes of another man in the Pend d'Oreille band. He accused me of making a baby with that man. He roared that you were not his daughter. That I was a whore. He swung his club and that was the end. You were only two sleeps old."

I feel sick. I back away, gagging, dry heaves seizing my body. The nausea passes, turns to fury. I grab the war club, clutch it with both hands and start off toward the shadow of the boulder.

Mother's voice stops me. "That war club is useless here. You cannot kill a spirit-being. Besides, Ironhand was not wrong. The gray-eyed man, Moonlight, was your real father. He was my true love—my only love—before being forced to marry Ironhand."

The club slips from my hands and falls at my feet.

"You have been blaming yourself for many things." Snow-Cave Man's voice. He is standing beside me. "It is time to let those things go."

"The hole in your memory is filled." Otter Woman speaks into my other ear.

"You were a woman of many gifts from Jésu." Snow-Cave Man again. "When you used those gifts to care for horses, to follow your calling, to help others, you walked a holy path. When you used those gifts to please your Father, to aid his lying and cheating, to compete for his favor against your brother and sister, you walked the devil's path."

Otter Woman continues. "Your love for Charges Ahead. Sometimes it was heart love, caring about him, praying for his safety, wanting a life together as help mates. At other times, your courtship was a way to bring wealth to your father, to seek his favor. You failed to understand how your father was using you."

I nod, sink to the sand between them. My life story is now clear. So many mistakes, so many sins. This is my punishment. Spending forever here in this place, with my father. I turn back toward the chasm. Mother is no longer present. Returned to the Great Beyond. My Lena, I will never find. I am a stone sinking into the abyss.

"Everyone's life is a mix of good and bad," Snow-Cave Man says.

"No one's life is perfect," Otter Woman says.

"Except Jésu," Snow-Cave Man says.

"Even gods make mistakes," Otter Woman says, smiling.

They chuckle, sharing what appears to be another unresolved debate.

"The important thing is to know your mistakes," Otter Woman says.

"Resolve to not repeat them," Snow-Cave Man says.

"It is never too late to change," Otter Woman tells me.

Snow-Cave Man nods and smiles.

I blink up at them. "But I am no longer alive. I cannot change now."

"That is what we once thought," Otter Woman says.

"Your journey has just begun," Snow-Cave Man says.

They pull me to my feet.

"Come." We will be your guides.

A sound of rushing water, I open my eyes. I am standing before a waterfall. The top is high up, hidden in a bank of clouds. The cascade splashes into a pool at my feet, from which flows a stream some twenty paces wide. The water, the clouds, the mossy ground on which I stand, are shades of purple. The smell of greenery and rich, black soil perfume the still air.

Something moves behind the waterfall. I realize there is an opening back there, a cave, or grotto. A figure steps into view, followed by a second. They circle the pool and walk, or float, toward me. Snow-Cave Man and Otter Woman.

I squeeze their hands, feeling a surge of hope.

"Where am I? Heaven? The Great Beyond?"

"Yet another stop along the way," Snow-Cave Man says.

"My daughter Lena. Is she here?"

A look passes between Snow-Cave man and Otter Woman, as if they are deciding who should answer.

Finally, Snow-Cave Man says, "We do not know."

Otter women touches my face, trying to comfort me. Her touch only triggers my tears. I slump forward, feel her arms enfold me.

"You are not yet ready to seek your daughter," she says. "There are questions that need answering first."

My head jerks up. "What questions?"

"Let us start with this one: What good has come from your life?

Good? Coupling with Charges Ahead, causing him to lose his life? Treating So-chee and Little Bear as enemies? Losing a race that resulted in Father's downfall? Tricking Lena into returning to Denver City to stop her from running off with the Alexander boy?

I shake my head. "Nothing good."

As if reading my mind, Otter Woman says, "What about your love for Charges Ahead? It was good, as was his for you. You enriched his life, however short. Some crossover before ever knowing such love. His walk was to give his life to defend the Salish people. He died with honor, and he is in a good place.

"Your brother and sister chose their own path," Snow-Cave Man says. "You are not the one who caused them to make their bargain with Crazy Bones to poison Shy Bird. In the Falling-leaves Moon race you stopped your mare before the colic could take her. You saved her life. And later, through your many winters with Papín, then with Medina at the Crossing, you kept your vow to Jésu to never follow the racing way again."

They are trying hard to warm my heart, these two friends, with their talking-way. But the stone inside my chest will not crumble.

"Why then was I punished after my vow, my atonement? My little Rosita, my young son, Martin, both dead. My older son Antonio, run from home, never again to be seen. At each heart-wound I prayed to Jésu, kept my vow. Asked for strength. Then I lost my Lena. It was too much. I cursed the name of Jésu. Cursed the name of Amotken. Cursed Medina, my husband, and John Alexander, who wanted to take Lena from me. So many curses!"

"Yours is the blaming-way," Otter Woman says. "Amotken is not to blame. He gives us sunlight, moonglow, stars, earth, living things, rocks, rain. There are evil spirits that cause pain, not Amotken."

"The Devil is the Black-robe name for it," Snow-Cave Man says. "Jésu is the One who gives us strength to survive the bad things. When you help people, care for others, love them, that is Jésu's spirit in your heart."

Otter Woman again: "Did you not love your children? Your husbands? Take care of them, treat their sicknesses, help them along their spirit paths?

I think back on my life after leaving the Bitterroot, with Papín, Medina, my children. Keeping my vow. Yes, there was some good there. I did some things right. Atoned for my early sins.

But guilt badger digs at my gut. I was the one who used my talking-way to send Lena back to her Denver school one last time, as part of our getaway plan. To Denver City where the sickness seized her. I was the one who convinced her to leave our home at Mariano's Crossing, leave Medina and her young suitor to run away with me to the Bitterroot. If I had not done this, she would still be alive.

I explain all this to my two guides. Otter Woman gives me a searching look, takes my hand, and asks the question that I have not been brave enough to ask myself: "What was your purpose in pulling your daughter into your getaway plan? Why did you do it?"

I look away to avoid the old medicine-woman's probing eyes. I recall telling Lena my plan was for her own good, that she needed to leave her young suitor to avoid making the mistakes that I made, to continue her horse-spirit path, to seek honor and fame as a horse woman rather than throwing it away on a too-early marriage and a trapped life of raising children, only to have them die.

But the shadow on my heart knows there is more. I mind-journey back to Lena's triumphant horseriding in the Denver City parade. As I watch her, my chest swells with pride. Pride for her, yes. But underneath, the pride is for me. I can no longer hide it. Truth cracks me open like a duck egg. I slump down on the moss.

Lena's glory was my glory. The celebration of me. I was seeking my girlhood dreams through my daughter. She was my replacement.

I pretended to keep my vow by using her to break it.

My heart drops when I remember how I tricked her. Spoke to her with two-tongues so she would leave her John Alexander and come with me instead. *Will she forgive me? Will I be able to find her to ask?* She died an innocent. I will die a sinner.

For many years I believed in forgiveness. Now I think there will be no forgiveness for me. That I will go to a different place than she.

My guides await my answer. Their faces are expectant, welcoming. It is difficult to tell them something I am barely brave enough to tell myself. But I do. They listen, nod, smile.

"You have taken another step along your journey," Snow-Cave Man says.

"You know your own heart better now," Otter Woman says. "A hard thing to do."

They turn to go. Their forms begin to dissolve in the mist of the waterfall.

"Wait!" I cry out. "Where are you going? Please do not leave me!"

"Heaven," says Snow-Cave Man

"The Road of Many Stars," says Otter Woman. Once again they give each other that knowing smile.

"But where will I go?"

"Each of us creates our own afterlife in the spirit world," Snow-Cave Man says.

"You will find your way now that that you have opened your heart,but you must share your heart with Lena before you can continue much further," Otter Woman says.

There is practically nothing left of their forms except their outlines dissolving in the mist.

I try to stifle my panic. "But where is Lena?" I hear myself almost shrieking.

"Walk behind the waterfall," Otter Woman tells me as she vanishes.

Then they are gone. The only sound is that of falling water.

I rush behind the cascade and plunge into a dark opening. Blackness closes around me, but I stumble on. I see a light ahead. It grows larger and brighter as I push toward it.

I emerge into a light so intense I must close my eyes. I feel my body floating, a breathtaking weightlessness. Fear leaves me. I feel...at peace. Relief. It is overwhelming. Awed, I quaver out a question. "Lena?"

Silence. Then...is it my imagination, or do I hear, somewhere in the distance, a faint reply?

David Jessup

AUTHORS NOTE

This much is history: Takánsy was a real person who was born into the Flathead tribe along the Bitterroot River in Montana sometime in the early 1800s. She left her people to marry a French fur trader named Louis Papín and was later traded to Mariano Medina in 1844 for the substantial price of six horses and six blankets. The fictionalized account of this exchange is described in my novel, *Mariano's Choice*.

At the beginning of the Colorado gold rush in 1848, Takánsy and Medina settled on the Big Thompson River near Loveland, Colorado, where Medina established a successful trading post and stage stop known as Mariano's Crossing. The tragic death and secret burial of their daughter, Lena Medina, in 1872 is the subject of my first novel, *Mariano's Crossing*.

The Flathead people went to great lengths

to bring Jesuit "Black-robes" to their homeland, dispatching no less than four delegations to Saint Louis during the 1830s. Chief Big Face, Old Ignácio and Little Ignácio were involved in these efforts, which finally culminated in the visit of Father Pierre John de Smet in 1840.

The other characters in this book—Ironhand, Snow-cave Man, Otter Woman, Charges Ahead, and Takánsy's family members—are all fictional products of my efforts to add some flesh to history's bare bones in order to explain why Takánsy left her people and ended up, years later, grieving the death of her beloved daughter, Lena.

ABOUT THE AUTHOR

David M. Jessup grew up at Sylvan Dale Ranch in Loveland, Colorado, owned and run by his family since 1946. A history buff, he is passionate about preserving open space, battling invasive weeds, catching wild river trout on a fly, singing cowboy songs, and telling stories about the American West—some of them true. He and his wife Linda now live in Maryland exploring the world with their grandchildren.

David Jessup is a popular speaker at book clubs, schools and community organizations on topics such as cattle ranching, sustainable agriculture, land conservation, flood recovery (he's been through two floods on the Big Thompson River in Colorado), fiction writing and the history behind his novels. His talks are sponsored by the Heart-J Center for Experiential Learning, www.heartjcenter.org.

Mariano's Crossing, his first novel, was selected as one of three finalists for the Colorado Book Award in literary fiction. He also won first place for mainstream, character-driven fiction in the Rocky Mountain Fiction Writers Contest and was selected as a finalist in the Pacific Northwest Writers Contest and the Santa Fe Writers Project.

Jessup's blog, *Beef, Books and Boots*, contains stories of ranch life and reviews of his favorite books about the American West.

His website is www.davidmjessup.com.

The ranch website is www.sylvandale.com.

CPSIA information can be obtained
at www.ICGtesting.com
Printed in the USA
JSHW011114070121
10750JS00006B/112